"Remember, Ilian? You took up that burning flag, the fame of all Garathorm, and rode against Ymryl's force. I had taught you sword and shield and axe, and you put all my learning to splendid use, until only you and I of all our army remained alive upon the field."

"Ay, I remember," said Ilian to Katinka. "The humiliation I felt when Ymryl discovered our feminine sex, touched my body and said: 'You will rule beside me.'

"It was then I swore to slay him…"

MICHAEL MOORCOCK

THE CHAMPION OF GARATHORM

The Chronicles of Castle Brass
Volume II

BERKLEY BOOKS, NEW YORK

This Berkley Book contains the complete
text of the original edition.

THE CHAMPION OF GARATHORM

A Berkley Book / published by arrangement with
the author

PRINTING HISTORY
Originally published in
Great Britain by
Mayflower Books Ltd.
Dell edition / March 1981
Berkley edition / April 1985

ISBN: 0-425-07646-6

Then the Earth grew old, its landscapes
mellowing and showing signs of age, its
ways becoming whimsical and strange in
the manner of a man in his last years.
    —*The High History of the Runestaff*

And when this History was done there followed
it another. A Romance involving the same
participants in experiences perhaps even more
bizarre and awesome than the last. And again
the ancient Castle of Brass in the marshy
Kamarg was the centre for much of this action . . .
    —*The Chronicles of Castle Brass*

CONTENTS

BOOK ONE
DEPARTURES

1. Representations and Possibilities   11
2. Count Brass Goes A-Journeying   20
3. A Lady All in Armour   27
4. News From Beyond The Bulgar Mountains   35
5. Reluctantly—A Quest   47

BOOK TWO
A HOMECOMING

1. Ilian of Garathorm   73
2. Outlaws of a Thousand Spheres   85
3. A Meeting in the Forest   94
4. A Pact is Made   100
5. The Raid on Virinthorm   108
6. The Wrong Champion   117

BOOK THREE
A LEAVETAKING

1. Sweet Battle, Triumphant Vengeance   127
2. An Impossible Death   136
3. The Swaying of the Balance   145
4. The Soul Gem   151

BOOK ONE
DEPARTURES

CHAPTER ONE

REPRESENTATIONS AND POSSIBILITIES

Dorian Hawkmoon was no longer mad, yet neither was he healthy. Some said that it was the Black Jewel which had ruined him when it had been torn from his forehead. Others said that the war against the Dark Empire had exhausted him of all the energy he would normally need for a full lifetime and that now there was no more energy left. And some would have it that Hawkmoon mourned for the love of Yisselda, Count Brass's daughter, who had died at the Battle of Londra. In the five years of his madness Hawkmoon had insisted that she was still alive, that she lived with him at Castle Brass and bore him a son and a daughter.

But while causes might be the subject of debate in the inns and taverns of Aigues-Mortes, the town which sheltered beneath the great Castle of Brass, the effects themselves were plain to all.

Hawkmoon brooded.

Hawkmoon pined and shunned human company, even that of his good friend Count Brass. Hawkmoon sat alone in a small room at the top of the castle's highest tower and, with chin on fist, stared out over the marshes, the fields of reeds, the lagoons, his eyes fixed not on the wild white bulls, the horned horses or the giant scarlet flamingoes of the Kamarg, but upon a distance, profound and numinous.

Hawkmoon tried to recall a dream or an insane fantasy. He tried to remember Yisselda. He tried to remember the names of the children he had imagined while he had been mad. But Yisselda was a shadow and he could see nothing of the children at all. Why did he yearn? Why was he full of such a deep and lasting sense of loss? Why did he sometimes nurse the thought that this, which he experienced now, was madness and that the dream—that of Yisselda and the children—had been the reality?

Hawkmoon no longer knew himself and had lost the inclination, as a result, to communicate with others. He was a ghost. He haunted his own apartments. A sad ghost who could only sob and groan and sigh.

At least he had been proud in his madness, said the townsfolk. At least he had been complete in his delusions.

'He was happier mad.'

Hawkmoon would have agreed with such sentiments, had they been expressed to him.

When not in the tower he haunted the room where he had set up his War Tables—high benches on which rested models of cities and castles occupied by thousands of other models of soldiers. In his madness he had commissioned this huge array from Vaiyonn, the local craftsman. To celebrate, he had told Vaiyonn, their victories over the Lords of Granbretan. And represented in painted metal were the Duke of Köln himself, Count Brass, Yisselda, Bowgentle, Huillam D'Averc and Oladahn of the Bulgar Mountains—the heroes of the Kamarg, most of whom had perished at Londra. And here too were models of their old enemies, the Beast Lords—Baron Meliadus in his wolf helm, King Huon in his Throne Globe, Shenegar Trott, Adaz Promp, Asrovak Mikosevaar and his wife, Flana (now

the gentle Queen of Granbretan). Dark Empire infantry, cavalry and flyers were ranged against the Guardians of the Kamarg, against the Warriors of Dawn,
against the soldiers of a hundred small nations.

And Dorian Hawkmoon would move all these pieces
about his vast boards, going through one permutation
after another; fighting a thousand versions of the same
battle in order to see how a battle which followed it
might have changed. And his heavy fingers were often
upon the models of his dead friends, and most of all
they were upon Yisselda. How could she have been
saved? What set of circumstances would have guaran-
teed her continuing to live?

Sometimes Count Brass would enter the room, his
eyes troubled. He would run his fingers through his grey-
ing red hair and watch as Hawkmoon, absorbed in his
miniature world, brought forward a squadron of cavalry
here, drew back a line of infantry there. Hawkmoon
either did not notice the presence of Count Brass on
these occasions or else he preferred to ignore his old
friend until Count Brass would clear his throat or otherwise make it evident that he had come in. Then Hawkmoon would look up, eyes introspective, bleak, unwel-
coming, and Count Brass would ask softly after Hawkmoon's health.

Hawkmoon would reply curtly that he was well.

Count Brass would nod and say that he was glad.

Hawkmoon would wait impatiently, anxious to get
back to his manoeuvrings on his tables, while Count
Brass looked around the room, inspected a battle-line or
pretended to admire the way Hawkmoon had worked
out a particular tactic.

Then Count Brass would say:

'I'm riding to inspect the towers this morning. It's a
fine day. Why don't you come with me, Dorian?'

Dorian Hawkmoon would shake his head. 'There are things I have to do here.'

'This?' Count Brass would indicate the wide trestles with a sweep of his hand. 'What point is there? They are dead. It is over. Will your speculation bring them back? You are like some mystic—some warlock—thinking that the facsimile can manipulate that which it imitates. You torture yourself. How can you change the past? Forget. Forget, Duke Dorian.'

But the Duke of Köln would purse his lips as if Count Brass had made a particularly offensive remark, and would turn his attention back to his toys. Count Brass would sigh, try to think of something to add, then he would leave the room.

Hawkmoon's gloom coloured the atmosphere of the whole Castle Brass and there were some who had begun to voice the opinion that, for all that he was a Hero of Londra, the duke should return to Germany and his traditional lands, which he had not visited since his capture, at the Bottle of Köln, by the Dark Empire lords. A distant relative now reigned as Chief Citizen there, presiding over a form of elected government which had replaced the monarchy of which Hawkmoon was the last living direct descendant. But it had never entered Hawkmoon's mind that he had any home other than his apartments in Castle Brass.

Even Count Brass would sometimes think, privately, that it would have been better for Hawkmoon if he had been killed at the Battle of Londra. Killed at the same time that Yisselda had been killed.

And so the sad months passed, all heavy with sorrow and useless speculation, as Hawkmoon's mind closed still more firmly around its single obsession until he hardly remembered to take sustenance or to sleep.

Count Brass and his old companion, Captain Josef

Vedla, debated the problem between themselves, but could arrive at no solution.

For hours they would sit in comfortable chairs on either side of the great fireplace in the main hall of Castle Brass, drinking the local wine and discussing Hawkmoon's melancholia. Both were soldiers and Count Brass had been a statesman, but neither had the vocabulary to cope with such matters as sickness of the soul.

'More exercise would help,' said Captain Josef Vedla one evening. 'The mind will rot in a body which does nothing. It is well known.'

'Aye—a healthy mind knows as much. But how do you convince a sick mind of the virtues of such action?' Count Brass replied. 'The longer he remains in his apartments, playing with those damned models, the worse he gets. And the worse he gets, the harder it is for us to approach him on a rational level. The seasons mean nothing to him. Night is no different to day for him. I shudder when I think what must be happening in his head!'

Captain Vedla nodded. 'He was never one for overmuch introspection before. He was a man. A soldier. Intelligent without being, as it were, *too* intelligent. He was practical. Sometimes it seems to me that he is a different man entirely now. As if the old Hawkmoon's soul was driven from its body by the terrors of the Black Jewel and a new soul entered to fill the place!'

Count Brass smiled at this. 'You're becoming fanciful, captain, in your old age. You praise the old Hawkmoon for being practical—and then make a suggestion like that!'

Captain Vedla was also forced to smile. 'Fair enough, Count Brass! Yet when one considers the powers of the old Dark Empire lords and remembers the powers of those who helped us in our struggle, perhaps the idea could have some foundation in terms of our own experience?'

'Perhaps. And if there were not more obvious answers to explain Hawkmoon's condition, I might agree with your theory.'

Captain Vedla became embarrassed, murmuring: 'It *was* merely a theory.' He raised his glass to catch the firelight, studying the rich, red wine within. 'And this stuff is doubtless what encourages me to voice such theories!'

'Speaking of Granbretan,' said Count Brass later, 'I wonder how Queen Flana is coping with the problem of the unregenerates who still, from what she has said in her letters, inhabit some of the darker, less accessible parts of underground Londra? I have had little news from her in recent months. I wonder if the situation has worsened, so that she devotes more time to it.'

'You have had a letter from her recently, surely?'

'By messenger. Two days ago. Aye. The letter was much briefer, however, than those she used to send. It was almost formal. Merely extending the usual invitation to visit her whenever I desired.'

'Could it be that, of late, she has become offended that you have not taken her up on her offer of hospitality?' Vedla suggested. 'Perhaps she thinks you do not feel friendship for her.'

'On the contrary, she is the nearest thing to my heart save for my memory of my own dead daughter.'

'But you have not indicated as much?' Vedla poured himself more wine. 'Women require these affirmations, you know. Even queens.'

'Flana is above such feelings. She is too intelligent. Too sensible. Too kind.'

'Possibly,' said Captain Vedla, as if he doubted Count Brass's words.

Count Brass understood the implication. 'You think I should write to her in more—more flowery terms?'

'Well . . .' Captain Vedla grinned.

'I was never capable of these literary flourishes.'

'Your style at its best (and on whatever subject) usually resembles communiques issued in the field during the heat of a battle,' Captain Vedla admitted. 'Though I do not mean that as an insult. On the contrary.'

Count Brass shrugged. 'I would not like Flana to think I did not remember her with anything but the greatest affection. Yet I cannot write. I suppose I should go to Londra—accept her offer.' He stared around his shadowed hall. 'It might be a change. This place has become almost overpoweringly gloomy of late.'

'You could take Hawkmoon with you. He was fond of Flana. It might be the only thing likely to attract him away from his toy soldiers.' Captain Vedla caught himself speaking sardonically and regretted it. He had every sympathy for Hawkmoon, every respect for him, even in his present state of mind. But Hawkmoon's brooding was a strain on all who had been even remotely connected with him in the past.

'I'll suggest it to him,' said Count Brass. Count Brass understood his own feelings. Much of him wanted to get away from Hawkmoon for a while. Yet his conscience would not let him go alone at least until he had put the idea to his old friend. And Vedla was right. A trip to Londra might force Hawkmoon out of his brooding mood. The chances were, however, that it would not. In which case, Count Brass anticipated a journey and a visit involving more emotional strain on himself and the rest of his party than that which they now experienced within the confines of Castle Brass.

'I'll speak to him in the morning,' Count Brass said

after a pause. 'Perhaps by returning to Londra itself, rather than by involving himself with models of the place, the melancholy in him will be exorcised . . .'

Captain Vedla agreed. 'It is something we should have considered earlier, maybe?'

Count Brass was, without rancour, thinking that Captain Vedla was expressing a certain amount of self-interest when he suggested that Hawkmoon go with him to Londra.

'And would you journey with us, Captain Vedla?' he asked with a faint smile.

'Someone would be needed here to act on your behalf . . .' Vedla said. 'However, if the Duke of Köln declined to go then, of course, I would be glad to accompany you.'

'I understand you, captain.' Count Brass leaned back in his chair, sipping his wine and regarding his old friend with a certain amount of humour.

After Captain Josef Vedla had left, Count Brass remained in his chair. He was still smiling. He cherished his amusement, for it had been a long while since he had felt any at all. And now that the idea was in his mind, he began to look forward to his visit to Londra, for he only realised at this moment to what extent the atmosphere had become oppressive in Castle Brass, once so famous for its peace.

He stared up at the smoke-darkened beams of the roof, thinking sadly of Hawkmoon and what he had become. He wondered if it was altogether a good thing that the defeat of the Dark Empire had brought tranquillity to the world. It was possible that Hawkmoon, even more than himself, was a man who only came alive when conflict threatened. If, for instance, there was trouble again in Granbretan—if the unregenerate remnants of the defeated warriors were seriously troubling Queen Flana—perhaps it would be a good notion to ask Hawkmoon to make it his business to find them and destroy them.

Count Brass sensed that a task of that nature would be the only thing which could save his friend. Instinctively he guessed that Hawkmoon was not made for peace. There were such men—men fashioned by fate to make war, either for good or for evil (if there was a difference between the two qualities)—and Hawkmoon might well be one of them.

Count Brass sighed and returned his attention to his new plan. He would write to Flana in the morning, sending news ahead of his intended visit. It would be interesting to see what had become of that strange city since he had last visited it, as a conqueror.

CHAPTER TWO

COUNT BRASS GOES A-JOURNEYING

'Give Queen Flana my kindest compliments,' said Dorian Hawkmoon distantly. He held a tiny representation of Flana in his pale fingers, turning the model this way and that as he spoke. Count Brass was not entirely sure that Hawkmoon realised he had picked the model up. 'Tell her that I do not feel fit enough to make the journey.'

'You would feel fitter once you had begun to travel,' Count Brass pointed out. He noticed that Hawkmoon had covered the windows with dark tapestries. The room was lit now by lamps, though it neared noon. And the place smelled dank, unhealthy, full of festering memories.

Hawkmoon rubbed at the scar on his forehead, where the Black Jewel had once been imbedded. His skin was waxy. His eyes burned with a dreadful, feverish light. He had become so thin that his clothes draped his body like drowned flags. He stood looking down at the table bearing the intricate model of old Londra, with its thousands of crazy towers, interconected by a maze of tunnels so that no inhabitant need ever see daylight.

Suddenly it occurred to Count Brass that Hawkmoon had caught the disease of those he had defeated. It would not have surprised the Count to discover that

Hawkmoon had taken to wearing an ornate and complicated mask.

'Londra has changed,' said Count Brass, 'since last you saw it. I hear that the towers have been torn down —that flowers grow in wide streets—that there are parks and avenues in place of the tunnels.'

'So I believe,' said Hawkmoon without interest. He turned away from Count Brass and began to move a division of Dark Empire cavalry out from beyond Londra's walls. He seemed to be working on a battle situation where the Dark Empire had defeated Count Brass and the other Companions of the Runestaff. 'It must be exceptionally—pretty. But for my own purposes I prefer to remember Londra as it was.' His voice became sharp, unwholesome. 'When Yisselda died there,' he said.

Count Brass wondered if Hawkmoon was blaming him—accusing him of cohabiting with those whose compatriots had slain Yisselda. He ignored the inference. He said: 'But the journey itself. Would that not be exhilarating? The last you saw of the outside world it was wasted, ruined. Now it flourishes again.'

'I have important things to do here,' Hawkmoon said.

'What things?' Count Brass spoke almost sharply. 'You have not left your apartments for months.'

'There is an answer,' Hawkmoon told him curtly, 'in all this. There is a way to find Yisselda.'

Count Brass shuddered.

'She is dead,' he said softly.

'She is alive,' Hawkmoon murmured. 'She is alive. Somewhere. In another place.'

'We once agreed, you and I, that there was no life after death,' Count Brass reminded his friend. 'Besides —would you resurrect a ghost. Would that please you— to raise Yisselda's shade?'

'If that were all I could resurrect, aye.'

'You love a dead woman,' Count Brass said in a quiet, disturbed voice. 'And in loving her you have fallen in love with death itself.'

'What is there in life to love?'

'Much. You would discover it again if you came with me to Londra.'

'I have no wish to see Londra. I hate the city.'

'Then just travel part of the distance with me.'

'No. I am dreaming again. And in my dreams I come closer to Yisselda—and our two children.'

'There never were children. You invented them. In your madness you invented them.'

'No. Last night I dreamed I had another name, but that I was still the same man. A strange, archaic name. A name from before the Tragic Millenium. John Daker. That was the name. And John Daker found Yisselda.'

Count Brass was close to weeping at his friend's insane mutterings. 'This reasoning—this dreaming—will bring you much more pain, Dorian. It will heighten the tragedy, not decrease it. Believe me. I speak the truth.'

'I know that you mean well, Count Brass. I respect your view and I understand that you believe that you are helping me. But I ask you to accept that you are not helping me. I must continue to follow this path. I know that it will lead me to Yisselda.'

'Aye,' said Count Brass sorrowfully. 'I agree. It will lead you to your death.'

'If that is the case, the prospect does not alarm me.' Hawkmoon turned again to regard Count Brass. The count felt a chill go through him as he looked at the gaunt, white face, the hot eyes which burned in deep sockets.

'Ah, Hawkmoon,' he said. 'Ah, Hawkmoon.'

And he walked towards the door and he said nothing else before he left the room.

And he heard Hawkmoon shout after him in a high, hysterical voice:

'I *will* find her, Count Brass!'

Next day Hawkmoon drew back the tapestry to peer through his window down into the courtyard below. Count Brass was leaving. His retinue was already mounted on good, big horses, caparisoned in the Count's red colours. Ribbons and pennants waved on holstered flame-lances, surcoats curled in the breeze, bright armour shone in the early morning sunlight. The horses snorted and stamped their feet. Servants moved about, making last minute preparations, handing warming drinks up to the horsemen. And then the Count Brass himself emerged and mounted his chestnut stallion, his brazen armour flickering as if fashioned from flame. The count looked up at the window, his face thoughtful for a moment. Then his expression changed as he turned to give an order to one of his men. Hawkmoon continued to watch.

While looking down upon the courtyard, he had been unable to rid himself of the sensation of observing particularly detailed models; models which moved and talked, yet were models nonetheless. He felt he could reach down and move a horseman to the other side of the courtyard, or pick up Count Brass himself and send him off away from Londra in another direction all together. He had vague feelings of resentment towards his old friend which he could not understand. Sometimes it occurred to him, in dreams, that Count Brass had bought his own life with that of his daughter. Yet how could that be? And neither was it a thing which Count Brass could possibly conceive of doing. On the contrary, the brave old warrior would have given his life for a loved one without a second thought. Still, Hawkmoon could not drive the thought from his skull.

For a moment he felt a pang of regret, wondering if he should, after all, have agreed to accompany Count Brass to Londra. He watched as Captain Josef Vedla rode forward and ordered the portcullis raised in the gateway. Count Brass had left Hawkmoon to rule in his place; but really the stewards and the veteran Guardians of the Kamarg could run things perfectly well and would make no demands on Hawkmoon for a decision.

But no, thought Hawkmoon. This was not a time for action, but a time for thought. He was determined to find a way through to those ideas which he could feel in the back of his own mind and yet which he could not, as yet, reach. For all his old friends might disdain his 'playing with toy soldiers' he knew that by putting the models through a thousand permutations it might release, at some point, those thoughts, those elusive notions which would lead him to the truth involving his own situation. And once he understood the truth, he was sure he would find Yisselda alive. He was almost sure, too, that he would find two children—perhaps a boy and a girl. They had all judged him mad for five years, yet he was convinced that he had not been mad. He believed that he knew himself too well—that if he ever did go mad it would not be in the way his friends had described.

Now Count Brass and his retinue were waving to the castle's retainers as they rode through the gates on the first stage of the long journey to Londra.

Contrary to Count Brass's suspicions, Dorian Hawkmoon still held his old friend in great esteem. It caused him a pang of sorrow to see Count Brass leaving. Hawk-

moon's problem was that he could no longer express any
of the sentiments he felt. He had become too single-
minded in his considerations, too absorbed in the problems which he attempted to solve in his obsessive
manipulation of the tiny figures on his boards.

Hawkmoon continued to watch as Count Brass and
his men rode down through the winding streets of
Aigues-Mortes. The streets were lined with townsfolk,
bidding Count Brass farewell. At last the party reached
the walls of the town and rode out across the broad
road through the marshes. Hawkmoon looked after them
until they were out of sight, then he turned his attention
back to his models.

Currently he was working out a situation in which
the Black Jewel had not been set in his forehead, but in
that of Oladahn of the Bulgar Mountains, and where
the Legion of the Dawn could not be summoned. Would
the Dark Empire have been defeated then? And if it
could have been defeated, how might that have been
accomplished? He had reached the point he had reached
a hundred times before, of re-enacting the Battle of
Londra. But this time it struck him that he, himself,
might have been killed. Would this have saved Yisselda's
life?

If he hoped, by going through these permutations of
past events, to find a means of releasing the truth he
believed to be hidden in his mind, he failed again. He
completed the tactics involved, he noted the fresh
possibilities involved, he considered his next develop-
ment. He wished that Bowgentle had not died at Londra.
Bowgentle had known much and might have helped him
in this line of reasoning.

There again, the messengers of the Runestaff—The
Warrior in Jet and Gold, Orland Fank or even the
mysterious Jehamia Cohnalias, who had not claimed to

be human—might have helped him. He had called to
them for their help in the darkness of the nights, but
they had not come. The Runestaff was safe now and
they had no need of Hawkmoon's help. He had felt
abandoned, though he knew they owed him nothing.

Yet could the Runestaff be involved in what had
happened to him, was happening to him now? Was that
strange artefact under some new threat? Had it set into
motion a fresh series of events, a new pattern of destiny?
Hawkmoon had a sense that there was more to his
situation than anything which the ordinary, observed
facts might suggest. He had been manipulated by the
Runestaff and its servants just as he now manipulated
his model soldiers. Was he being manipulated again?
And was that why he turned to the models, deceiving
himself that he controlled something when, in fact, he
was controlled?

He pushed such thoughts aside. He must devote himself to his original speculations.

And thus it was that he avoided confronting the truth.

By pretending to search for the truth, by pretending
that he was single-minded in that quest, he was able to
escape it. For the truth of his situation might have been
intolerable to him.

And that was ever the way of mankind.

CHAPTER THREE

A LADY ALL IN ARMOUR

A month went by.

Twenty alternative destinies were played out on Hawkmoon's wargame boards. And Yisselda came no closer to him, even in his dreams.

Unshaven, red-eyed, acned, his skin flaking with eczema, weak from lack of food, flabby from lack of exercise, Dorian Hawkmoon had nothing of the hero left in him, either in his mind, his character or his body. He looked thirty years older than his real age. His clothes, stained, torn, ill-smelling, were the clothes of a beggar. His unwashed hair hung in greasy strands about his face. His beard contained flecks of distasteful substances. He had taken to wheezing, to muttering to himself, to coughing. His servants avoided him as much as they could. He had little cause to call on them and so he did not notice their absence.

He had changed beyond recognition, this man who had been the Hero of Köln, the Champion of the Runestaff, the great warrior who had led the oppressed to victory over the Dark Empire.

And his life was fading from him, though he did not realise it.

In his obsession with alternative destinies he had come close to fixing his own; he was destroying himself.

And his dreams were changing. And because they

were changing he slept even less frequently than before. In his dreams he had four names. One of them was John Daker, but much more often now did he sense the other names—Erekosë and Urlik. Only the fourth name escaped him, though he knew it was there. On waking, he could never recall the fourth name. He began to wonder if there was such a thing as reincarnation. Was he remembering earlier lives? That was his instinctive conclusion. Yet his common sense could not accept the idea.

In his dreams he sometimes met Yisselda. In his dreams he was always anxious, always weighed down by a sense of heavy responsibility, of guilt. He always felt that it was his duty to perform some action, but could never recall what that action was. Had he lived other lives that had been just as tragic as this one? The thought of an eternity of tragedy was too much for him. He drove it off, almost before it had formed.

And yet these ideas were half-familiar. Where had he heard them before? In other, earlier dreams? In conversation with someone? With Bowgentle? In Danark, the distant city of the Runestaff?

He began to feel threatened. He began to know terror. Even the models on his tables were half-forgotten. He began to see shadows moving at the corners of his eyes.

What was causing the fear?

He thought that possibly he was close to understanding the truth concerning Yisselda and that there were certain forces pledged to stop him; forces which might kill him just as he was on the point of discovering how to reach her.

The only thing which Hawkmoon did not consider—the only answer which did not come to mind—was that his fear was, in fact, fear of himself, fear of facing an unpleasant truth. It was the lie which was threatened, the protecting lie and, as most men will, he fought to defend that lie, to stave off its attackers.

It was at this time that he began to suspect his servants of being in league with his enemies. He was sure that they had made attempts to poison him. He took to locking his doors and refusing to open them when servants came to perform some necessary function. He ate the barest amount necessary to keep alive. He collected rain water from the cups he set out on the sills of his windows and he drank only that water. Yet still fatigue would overwhelm his weakened body and then the little dreams would come to the man who dwelt in darkness. Dreams which in themselves were not unpleasant—gentle landscapes, strange cities, battles which Hawkmoon had never taken part in, peculiar, alien folk whom Hawkmoon had never encountered even in the strangest of his adventures in the service of the Runestaff. And yet they terrified him. Women appeared in those dreams, also, and some might have been Yisselda, yet he experienced no pleasure when he dreamed of these women, only a sense of deep disquiet. And once, fleetingly, he dreamed that he looked in a mirror and saw a woman there in place of his own reflection.

One morning he awoke from such a slumber and instead of rising, as was his habit, and going directly to his tables, he remained where he lay, looking up at the rafters of his room. In the dim light filtering through the tapestries across the window he could, quite plainly, see the head and shoulders of a man who bore a strong resemblance to the dead Oladahn. The resemblance was mostly in the way the head was held, in the expression, in the eyes. There was a wide-brimmed hat on the long, black hair and a small black and white cat sat on the shoulder. Hawkmoon noticed, without surprise, that the cat had a pair of wings folded neatly on its back.

'Oladahn?' Hawkmoon said, though he knew it was not Oladahn.

The face smiled and made as if to speak.

Then it had vanished.

Hawkmoon pulled dirty silk sheets over his head and lay there trembling. It began to dawn on him that he was going mad again, that perhaps Count Brass had been right, after all, and that he had experienced hallucinations for five years.

Later Hawkmoon got up and uncovered his mirror. Some weeks before he had thrown a robe over the mirror, for he had not wished to see himself.

He looked at the wretch who peered back at him through the dusty glass.

'I see a madman,' Hawkmoon murmured. 'A dying madman.'

The reflection aped the movement of the lips. The eyes were frightened. Above them, in the centre of the forehead, was a pale scar, perfectly circular, where once a black jewel had burned, a jewel which could eat a man's brain.

'There are other things which eat at a man's brain,' muttered the Duke of Köln. 'Subtler things than jewels. Worse things than jewels. How cleverly, after they are dead, do the Dark Empire lords reach out to take vengeance on me. By slaying Yisselda they brought slow death to me.'

He covered the mirror again and sighed a thin sigh. Painfully he walked back to his couch and sat down again, not daring to look up at the ceiling where he had seen the man who so much resembled Oladahn.

He was reconciled to the fact of his own wretched-
ness, his own death, his own madness. Weakly, he
shrugged.

'I was a soldier,' he said to himself. 'I became a fool.
I deceived myself. I thought I could achieve what great
scientists and sorcerers achieve, what philosophers
achieve. And I was never capable of it. Instead, I turned
myself from a man of skill and reason into this diseased
thing which I have become. And listen. Listen, Hawkmoon. You are talking to yourself. You mutter. You
rave. You whine. Dorian Hawkmoon, Duke von Köln,
it is too late for you to redeem yourself. You rot.'

A small smile crossed his sick lips.

'Your destiny was to fight, to carry a sword, to perform the rituals of war. And now tables have become
your battle-fields and you have lost the strength to bear
a dirk, let alone a sword. You could not sit a horse if
you wished to.'

He let himself drop back onto his soiled pillow. He
covered his face with his arms. 'Let the creatures come,'
he said. 'Let them torment me. It is true. I am mad.'

He started, believing he heard someone groaning beside him. He forced himself to look.

It was the door which groaned. A servant had pushed
it open. The servant stood nervously in the opening.

'My lord?'

'Do they all say I am mad, Voisin?'

'My lord?'

The servant was an old man, one of the few who
still regularly attended Hawkmoon. He had served
Hawkmoon ever since the Duke of Köln had first come
to Castle Brass. Yet there was a nervous look in his eyes
as he replied.

'Do they, Voisin?'

Voisin spread his hands. 'Some do, my lord. Others say you are unwell—a physical disease. I have felt for sometime that perhaps a doctor could be called . . .'

Hawkmoon felt a return of his old suspicions. 'Doctors? Poisoners?'

'Oh, no, my lord!'

Hawkmoon controlled himself. 'No, of course not. I appreciate your concern, Voisin. What have you brought me?'

'Nothing, my lord, save news.'

'Of Count Brass? How fares Count Brass in Londra?'

'Not of Count Brass. Of a visitor to Castle Brass. An old friend of the count's, I understand, who, on hearing that Count Brass was absent and that you were undertaking his responsibilities, asked to be received by you.'

'By me?' Hawkmoon smiled grimly. 'Do they know what I have become, in the outside world?'

'I think not, my lord.'

'What did you tell them?'

'That you were not well but that I would convey the message.'

'And that you have done.'

'Aye, my lord, I have.' Voisin hesitated. 'Shall I say that you are indisposed . . .?'

Hawkmoon began to nod assent but then changed his mind, pushing himself from the bed and standing up. 'No. I will receive them. In the hall. I will come down.'

'Would you wish to—to prepare yourself, my lord? Toilet things—some hot water?'

'No. I will join our guest in a few minutes.'

'I will take your decision to them.' Rather hastily Voisin departed from Hawkmoon's apartments, plainly disturbed by Hawkmoon's decision.

* * *

Deliberately, maliciously, Hawkmoon made no attempt to improve his appearance. Let his visitor see him as he was.

Besides, he was most certainly mad. Even this could be one of his fantasies. He could be anywhere—in bed, at his tables, even riding through the marshes—and only believing that these events were taking place. As he left his bed-chamber and passed through the room in which his model tables had been set up, he brushed at ranks of soldiers with his dirty sleeves, he knocked over buildings, he kicked at a leg so that an earthquake took place in the city of Köln.

He blinked as he came out onto the landing, lit by huge, tinted windows at both ends. The light hurt his eyes.

He walked towards the stairs which wound down to the great hall. He clutched a rail, feeling dizzy. His own infirmity amused him. He looked forward to his visitor's shock when he appeared.

A servant hurried up to help him and he leaned heavily on the young man's arm as, slowly, they descended.

And at last he reached the hall.

An armoured figure stood admiring one of Count Brass's battle trophies—a lance and a dented shield which he had won off Orson Kach during the Rhine Cities Wars, many years before.

Hawkmoon did not recognize the figure at all. It was fairly short, stocky and had a somewhat belligerent stance. Some old fighting companion of the count's, when he was a mercenary general, almost certainly.

'Greetings,' wheezed Hawkmoon. 'I am the present custodian of Castle Brass.'

The figure turned. Cool, grey eyes looked Hawkmoon up and down. There was no shock in the eyes, no expression at all as the figure stepped forward, hand extended.

Indeed, it was likely that Hawkmoon's own face betrayed surprise, at very least.

For his visitor, dressed all in battered armour, was a middle-aged woman.

'Duke Dorian?' she said. 'I am Katinka van Bak. I've been travelling many nights.'

CHAPTER FOUR

NEWS FROM BEYOND
THE BULGAR MOUNTAINS

'I was born in sea-drowned Hollandia,' said Katinka van Bak, 'though my mother's parents were traders from Muskovia. In the battles between our country and the Belgic States, my kin were slain and I became a captive. For a while I served—in a manner you can imagine—in the retinue of Prinz Lobkowitz of Berlin. He had aided the Belgics in their war and I was part of his spoil.' She paused to take another slice of cold beef from the plate before her. Her armour was discarded and she wore a simple silk shirt and a pair of blue cotton breeks. For all she leaned her arms on the table and spoke in blunt, unladylike tones, she was not unfeminine and Hawkmoon found himself liking her very much.

'Well, I spent much time in the company of warriors and it became my ambition to learn their skills. It amused them to teach me to use sword and bow and I continued to affect an awkwardness with weapons long after I had mastered their use. In this means I succeeded in not arousing any suspicion as to my plans.'

'You planned to escape?'

'A little more than that.' Katinka van Bak smiled and wiped her lips. 'There came a time when Prinz Lobkowitz himself heard of my eccentricity. I remember his laughter when he was taken to the quadrangle outside the dormitories where we girls lived. The soldier who had made me his special protégé gave me a sword and we duelled, he and I, for a while, to demonstrate to the prince the charming artlessness with which I thrust and parried. This was fine amusement indeed and Prinz Lobkowitz said that as he was entertaining guests that evening it would be a novel idea to show me off to them, something to make a change from the usual jongleurs and such who normally performed at such functions. This suited me well. I fluttered my lashes and smiled shyly and pretended to be pleased that I had been granted such an honour—pretended that I did not realise they were all laughing at me.'

Hawkmoon tried to imagine Katinka van Bak fluttering her lashes and playing the ingenue, but the effort defeated his imagination. 'And what happened?' He was genuinely curious. For the first time in months something was happening to take his attention away from his own problems. He rested an unshaven chin on a scabrous hand as Katinka van Bak continued.

'Well, that evening I was presented to the delighted guests who watched me girlishly duelling with several of Prinz Lobkowitz's warriors. They ate much as they watched, but they drank more. Several of the prince's guests—men and women—offered to buy me for large sums and this, of course, increased Prinz Lobkowitz's pride that he owned me. Naturally, he refused to sell. I remember his calling out to me:

' "And now, little Katinka, how many other martial arts do you pursue? What will you show us next?"

'Judging my moment to be the right one, I curtseyed prettily and, as if with naive boldness, said:

' "I have heard that you are a great swordsman, Your Grace. The best in all the province of Berlin."

' "So it is said," replied Lobkowitz.

' "Would you do me the honour of crossing swords with me, my lord? So that I may test my skill against the finest blade in this hall?"

'Prince Lobkowitz was taken aback by this at first, but then he laughed. It was hard for him to refuse in front of his guests, as I'd known. He decided to indulge me, but said gravely:

' "In Berlin there are different stakes for different forms of duelling. We fight for a first body-cut, for a first cut on the left cheek, for a first cut on the right cheek and so on—up to duelling to the death. I would not like to spoil your beauty, little Katinka."

' "Then let us fight to the death, Your Grace!" I said, as if carried away by the reception I had received.

'Laughter filled the hall, then. But I saw many an eager eye looking from me to the prince. None doubted that the prince would win any duel, of course, but they would be gratified at seeing my blood spilled.

'Lobkowitz was nonplussed, too drunk to think clearly, to work out the implications of my suggestion. But he did not wish to lose face in front of his guests.

' "I would not kill such a talented slave," he said jovially. "I think we should consider some other stake, little Katinka."

' "My freedom, then?" I suggested.

' "Neither would I lose so entertaining a girl . . ." he began. But then the crowd was roaring at him to take more sporting an attitude. After all, they all knew he would play with me for a while before delivering a token cut or disarming me.

' "Very well!" He smiled and shrugged and accepted a blade from one of his guards, stepping from his table to the floor and taking up a fighting stance before me.

"Let's begin." I could see that he intended to display his own skill in the manner in which he would prolong the duel.

'The fight began clumsily enough. Awkwardly I thrust and insouciantly he parried. The crowd of guests cheered me on and some even began to make wagers on how long the duel would last—though none wagered that I would win, of course.' Katinka van Bak poured a cup of apple juice for herself and swallowed it down before going on with her story.

'As you have guessed, Duke Dorian, I had become a swordswoman of no mean ability. Slowly I began to reveal my talent and slowly it dawned on Prinz Lobkowitz that he was having to use more and more of his skill to defend himself. I could see that he was beginning to realise that he fought an opponent who might well be his match. The idea of being beaten by a slave—and a slave-girl, at that—was not a pleasant one. He began to fight seriously. He wounded me twice. Once in the left shoulder and once in the thigh. But I fought on. And now, I recall, there was absolute silence in the hall, save for the sound of our steel and of Prinz Lobkowitz's heavy breathing. We fought for an hour. He would have killed me if he could.'

'I remember,' said Hawkmoon, 'a tale I heard when I ruled in Köln. So you are the woman who . . . ?'

'Who slew the Prince of Berlin? Aye. I killed him in his own hall, before his own guests, in the presence of his own bodyguards. I took him in his heart with a single clean thrust. He was the first I killed. And before they could believe what they had seen I had raised my sword and reminded them all of the prince's bargain—that if I won the duel I should have my freedom. I doubt if any of the prince's close retainers would have kept

that bargain. They would have slain me there and then
if it had not been for Lobkowitz's friends and those who
had had ambitions upon his territories. Several of them
gathered round me to offer me positions in their house-
holds—as a novelty, you understand, rather than for my
battle-skill. I accepted a post in the guard of Guy
O'Pointte, Archduke of Bavaria. On the spot. The
archduke's guard was the largest there, you understand, since he was the most powerful of the nobles
assembled. After that, the dead prince's men decided
to honour their master's bargain.'

'And that is how you became a soldier?'

'Aye. Eventually I became Guy O'Pointte's chief
general. When the archduke was murdered by his uncle's family, I left the service of Bavaria and went to
find a new position. And that, of course, is when I met
Count Brass. We've served as mercenaries together in
half the armies of Europe—and often on the same side!
At about the time your count settled here in the Kamarg, I went east and joined the permanent service of
the Prince of Ukrainia, where I advised him on the re-
construction of his army. We put a good defence
against the legions of the Dark Empire.'

'You were captured by the Beast Lords?'

Katinka van Bak shook her head. 'I escaped to the
Bulgar Mountains, where I remained until after you and
your comrades had turned the tables on them at the
Battle of Londra. It fell upon me to help restore
Ukrainia, the prince's youngest niece being the only
surviving member of the family. I became Regent of
Ukrainia, through no particular wish of my own.'

'You have renounced that position, then? Or are you
merely visiting us incognito?'

'I did not renounce the position and I am not visiting

you incognito,' said Katinka van Bak firmly, as if chiding
Hawkmoon for trying to hurry her in her story. 'Ukrainia
was invaded.'

'What? By whom? I thought the world at relative
peace!'

'So it is. Or was until a short time ago when we who
dwell to the east of the Bulgar Mountains began to hear
of an army which had gathered in those mountains.'

'The Dark Empire resurgents!'

Katinka van Bak held up a chiding hand to silence
him.

'It was a rabble army,' she went on. 'Certainly it was
that. But I do not think it was the remains of the Dark
Empire army. Though it was vast and had powerful
weapons at its disposal, no individual comprising it resembled another. They wore different styles of clothing,
carried different kinds of weapons, belonged to different
races—some of which were by no means human. Do
you follow me—each one looked as if he belonged to a
different army!'

'A band comprised of soldiers who survived the conquerings of the Dark Empire?'

'I think not. I do not know where these came from.
All I do know is that every time they ventured from
their mountains—which they had made their own and
turned them into an impregnable fortress—almost—no
expedition ever sent against this army was ever successful. Each force was wiped out. They kill whole popula-
tions—to the last new-born baby—and strip villages,
cities, whole nations of everything of value. In that respect they are like bandits, rather than an organised
army with some ultimate purpose. These seem to attack countries for loot alone. And as a result they ex-
tend their activities further and further, returning al-

ways with their booty, their stolen food and—very occasionally—women, to their mountain stronghold.'

'Who leads them?'

'I know not, though I've fought them when they
came against the Ukraine. Either several lead them or
none does. There is no-one to reason with, to parley
with. They seem moved only by greed and a lust to kill.
They are like locusts. There is no other description
which fits them better. Even the Dark Empire allowed
survivors, for it planned to rule the world and needed
people to serve it. But these—these are worse.'

'It's hard to conceive of an aggressor worse than the
Dark Empire,' said Hawkmoon feelingly. 'But,' he added
quickly, 'I believe you, of course, Katinka van Bak.'

'Aye, believe me, for I'm the sole survivor. I thank
the life I've led. It has given me the experience to know
when a situation is lost and how to escape the consequences of such a loss. No other creature remains alive
in Ukrainia or many other lands beyond the Bulgar
Mountains.'

'So you fled to warn the lands this side of the mountains? To raise an army, perhaps, against this powerful
rabble?'

'I fled. That is all. I have told my story to anyone
who will listen, but I do not expect much will be done
as a result. Most will not care what has happened to
folk dwelling in such distant parts, even if they believed
me in the first place. Therefore, to try to raise an army
would be fruitless. And, I'll add, any human army which
went against those who now occupy the Bulgar Mountains would be utterly destroyed.'

'Will you go on to Londra? Count Brass will be there
by now.'

Katinka van Bak sighed and stretched. 'Not immediately, I think. If at all. I am weary. I have been rid-

ing almost without pause since leaving Ukrainia. If you do not object, I'll remain at Castle Brass until my old friend returns. Unless I have a whim to continue on to Londra. At the moment, however, I have no inclination to move beyond these walls.'

'You are, of course, fully welcome,' said Hawkmoon eagerly. 'It is an honour for me. You must tell me more of your tales of the old days. And you must give me your theories about this rabble army—where it might have come from, and so on.'

'I have no ideas on that subject,' said Katinka van Bak. 'There is no logical explanation. They appeared overnight and have been there ever since. Discourse with them is impossible. It is like attempting to talk reasonably to a hurricane. There is a sense of desperation about them, a wild contempt for their own lives as well as yours. And the clothing and forms of the soldiers, as I have said, is so disparate. Not one alike. And yet, you know, I thought I recognised one or two familiar faces in the throng which swept over us. Soldiers I'd known who had been dead these many years since. And I'll swear I saw Count Brass's old friend, Bowgentle, riding with them. Yet I heard Bowgentle was killed at Londra . . .'

'He was. He was. I saw his remains.' Hawkmoon, whose interest up until now had been relatively faint, now became eager to hear all Katinka van Bak could tell him. He felt he was on the verge of solving the problem he had been working on all this time. Perhaps he had not been so insane, after all. 'Bowgentle, you say. And others who were familiar—yet dead?'

'Aye.'

'Did any women ride in the army?'

'Yes. Several.'

'Any you recognised . . .?' Hawkmoon leaned across the table, staring intensely at Katinka van Bak.

She frowned, trying to recall, then she shook her head so that her grey braids swung. 'No.'

'Not Yisselda, perhaps? Yisselda of Brass?'

'She who died at Londra, too?'

'So it's said.'

'No. Besides I should not have recognised her. She was a small child when last I saw her.'

'Ah,' said Hawkmoon, resuming his chair. 'Yes. I forgot.'

'That is not to say she could not have been there,' went on the warrior woman. 'There were so many. I did not see half the army which conquered me.'

'Well, if you recognised Bowgentle, perhaps all the others were there—all those who died at Londra?'

'I said I thought the man I saw resembled Bowgentle. But why should Bowgentle or anyone else who was a friend of yours ride in such an army?'

'True.' Hawkmoon drew his brows together in thought. His eyes had lost their dullness. His movements had become somewhat more energetic. 'Say that he and the others were charmed, perhaps. In trances. Forced to do the will of an enemy. The Dark Empire had powers which could make such a thing possible.'

'It is fanciful, Duke Dorian . . .'

'As would sound the History of the Runestaff, if we did not know it to be true.'

'I agree, but . . .'

'I have long cherished an instinct, you see,' Hawkmoon told her, 'that Yisselda did not die at Londra, for all there were many witnesses to her death and burial. It is also possible that none of our other friends died at Londra—that all were victims of some secret Dark Em-

pire counterplan. Could not the Dark Empire have sub-
stituted bodies for Yisselda and the rest, then borne the
real people away to the Bulgar Mountains—captured
others, too? Could you not have fought an army of
Dark Empire slaves, controlled by those who escaped
our vengeance?'

'But so few did escape. And none of the Lords lived
after the Battle of Londra. So who could be making such
plans, even if they were likely. Which they most de-
cidedly are not, Duke Dorian.' Katinka van Bak pursed
her lips. 'I thought you a man of sense. A practical
soldier, like myself.'

'I thought so once—until this idea came into my mind
—that Yisselda still lives. Somewhere.'

'I had heard that you were not wholly your old
self . . .'

'You mean that you had heard I was mad. Well,
madam, I do believe I am mad. Perhaps I have indulged
in mad follies, of late, but only because the idea—the
central idea—has truth in it.'

'I accept what you say,' said Katinka van Bak evenly.
'But I would need considerable proof of such a theory.
I do not have an instinct that the dead live . . .'

'I think Count Brass has,' Hawkmoon told her.
'Though he would not admit it. I think it is something he refuses to consider for he fears that he would
go as mad as he thought me to be.'

'And that could also be,' agreed Katinka van Bak,
'but again I have no evidence that Count Brass thinks
as you say. I should have to meet him again and talk
with him in order to test your words.'

Hawkmoon nodded. He thought for a moment and
then said:

'But suppose I have a means of defeating this army?
What would you say? If my theories led me to the

truth concerning the army and its origins and that they, in turn, led me to an understanding of its weaknesses.'

'Then your theories would be in a practical direction,' Katinka van Bak said. 'But unfortunately there is only one way to test them and that involves losing one's life if one is wrong. Eh?'

'I would willingly take that risk. When I fought the Dark Empire I soon realised there was no way to overcome it by direct confrontation, but if one sought weaknesses in the leaders, and made use of those weaknesses, then they could be defeated. That is what I learned in the service of the Runestaff.'

'You think you know how to defeat that rabble?' Katinka van Bak was by now half-convinced.

'Obviously I do not know the exact nature of the weakness. But I could discover it probably better than anyone else in the world!'

'I think you could!' exclaimed Katinka van Bak, grinning. 'I'm with you there. But I think it is too late to look for weaknesses.'

'If I could observe them. If I could find a hiding place, perhaps in the mountains themselves, and watch them, then perhaps I could think of a way of defeating them.' Hawkmoon was thinking of another thing he might gain from observing the rabble army, but he kept that idea to himself. 'You hid in those same mountains for a long while, Katinka van Bak. You, better than anyone save Oladahn himself, could find me a lair from which I might spy on the locusts!'

'I could, but I have just fled from those parts. I have no wish to lose my life, young man, as I told you. Why should I take you into the Bulgar Mountains, the very stronghold of my enemies?'

'Had you not nursed at least a little hope that your Ukrainia might be avenged? Did you not think to yourself, even secretly, that you might enlist the help of Count Brass and his Kamargians against your foes?'

Katinka van Bak smiled. 'Well, I knew the hope to be foolish, but . . .'

'And now I offer you a chance of taking that vengeance. All you need do is lead me into the mountains, find me a place that is relatively safe, and then you could even depart if you wished.'

'Are your motives selfless, Duke Dorian?'

Hawkmoon hesitated. Then he admitted: 'Perhaps not wholly selfless. I wish to test my theory that Yisselda still lives and that I can save her.'

'Then I think I'll take you to the Bulgar Mountains,' said Katinka van Bak. 'I do not trust a man who tells me that anything he does is completely selfless. But I think I can trust you.'

'I think you can,' said Hawkmoon.

'The only problem that I can see,' added the warrior woman frankly, 'is whether you'll survive the journey. You are in extremely poor condition, you know.' She reached forward and fingered his garments just as if she were a peasant woman buying a goose in the market. 'You need fattening up for a start. Let a week pass first. Get some food into your belly. Exercise. Ride. We'll have a mock duel or two together . . .'

Hawkmoon smiled. 'I am glad that you hold no grudge against me, my lady, or I should think twice about accepting that last suggestion at face value!'

And Katinka van Bak flung back her head and laughed.

CHAPTER FIVE

RELUCTANTLY — A QUEST

Hawkmoon ached in every limb. He made a sorry sight as he stumbled out into the courtyard where Katinka van Bak already waited, mounted on a frisky stallion whose hot breath clouded the early morning air. Hawkmoon's mount was a less nervous beast, but known for his reliability and stamina, yet Hawkmoon did not relish the prospect of climbing into the animal's saddle. His stomach was griping him, his head swam, his legs shook, for all that he had spent more than a week exercising and eating a good diet. His appearance had improved a little, and he was cleaner, but he was not the Runestaff Hero who had ridden out against Londra only seven years earlier. He shivered, for winter was beginning to touch the Kamarg. He wrapped his heavy leather cloak about him. The cloak was lined with wool and was almost too warm when closed. So heavy was the cloak that it almost bore him to the ground as he walked. He carried no weapons. His sword and flame-lance were in saddle scabbards. He wore, as well as the cloak, a thick quilted jerkin of dark red, doeskin leggings stitched with complicated designs by Yisselda, when she lived, and plain knee-boots of good, gleaming leather. Upon his head was a simple helmet. Aside from this, he wore no armour. He was not strong enough to wear armour.

Hawkmoon was still not healthy, either in mind or body. What had driven him to improve his physical condition to this degree had not been disgust with what he had become but his insane belief that he might find Yisselda alive in the Bulgar Mountains.

With some difficulty, he mounted his horse. Then he was bidding farewell to his stewards, completely forgetful that Count Brass had left the responsibility of running the province in his hands, and following Katinka van Bak through the gates and down through the empty streets of Aigues-Mortes. No citizens lined these streets. None, save the servants at the castle, knew that he was leaving Castle Brass, heading east where Count Brass had headed west.

By noon the two figures had passed through the reed-fields, passed the marshes and the lagoons, and were following a hard white road past one of the great stone towers which marked the borders of the land of which Count Brass was Lord Protector.

Weary of riding even this comparatively short distance, Hawkmoon was beginning to regret his decision. His arms ached from clinging to his saddle pommel, his thighs gave him agonising pain and his legs had gone completely numb. Katinka van Bak, on the other hand, seemed tireless. She kept stopping her own horse to allow Hawkmoon to catch up, yet was deaf to his suggestions that they stop and rest for a while. Hawkmoon wondered if he would last the journey, if he would not die on the way to the Bulgar Mountains. He wondered, from time to time, how he could ever have conceived a liking for this fierce, heartless woman.

They were hailed by a Guardian who saw them from his post at the top of the tower. His riding flamingo stood beside him and his scarlet cloak waved in the

breeze so that for a moment Hawkmoon saw man and
bird as one creature. The Guardian raised his long
flame-lance in salute as he recognised Hawkmoon.
Hawkmoon managed to wave a feeble hand in return,
but was unable to call back in reply to the Guardian's
greeting.

Then the tower had dwindled behind them as they
took the road to Lyonesse, with a view to skirting the
Switzer Mountains which were said to be tainted still
with the poisons of the Tragic Millenium and which
were, besides, all but impassable. Also, in Lyonesse
Katinka van Bak had acquaintances who would give
them provisions for the remainder of their journey.

They camped on the road that night and in the
morning Hawkmoon had become fully convinced of his
own imminent death. The pain of the previous day was
as nothing with the agony he felt now. Katinka van Bak,
however, continued to show no mercy, heaving him per-
emptorily upon his patient horse before climbing into
her own saddle. Then she grasped his bridle and led
horse and swaying rider after her.

Thus they progressed for three more days, hardly
resting at all, until Hawkmoon collapsed altogether,
falling from his saddle in a faint. He no longer cared
whether he found Yisselda or not. He neither blamed
nor condoned Katinka van Bak for her ruthless treat-
ment of his person. His pain had faded to a perpetual
ache. He moved when the horse moved. He stopped
when the horse stopped. He ate the food which Katinka
van Bak would occasionally put in front of him. He
slept for the few hours she allowed him. And then he
fainted.

He woke once and opened his eyes to receive a view
of his own swaying feet on the other side of his horse's

belly, and he knew that Katinka van Bak continued her journey, having slung him over the saddle of his own steed.

It was in this manner, some time later, that Dorian Hawkmoon, Duke von Köln, Champion of the Runestaff, Hero of Londra, entered the old city of Lyon, capital of Lyonesse, his horse led by an old woman in dusty armour.

And the next time Dorian Hawkmoon woke he lay in a soft bed and there were young maidens bending over him, smiling at him, offering him food. He refused to accept their existence for some moments.

But they were real and the food was good and the rest revived him.

Two days later the reluctant Hawkmoon, in considerably better condition now, left with Katinka van Bak to continue their quest for the rabble army of the Bulgar Mountains.

'You're filling out at last, lad,' said Katinka van Bak one morning as they rode into the sun which was turning to a glowing green the rolling, gentle hills of the land through which they travelled. She rode beside him now, no longer finding it necessary to lead his horse. She slapped him on the shoulder. 'You've good bones. There was nothing wrong with you that couldn't be put right, as you see.'

'Health achieved through such an ordeal as that, madam,' said Hawkmoon feelingly, 'is scarcely worth attaining.'

'You'll feel grateful to me yet.'

'I tell you honestly, Katinka van Bak, I am not sure I shall!'

And at this Katinka van Bak, Regent of Ukrainia, laughed heartily and spurred her stallion along the narrow track through the grass.

Hawkmoon was forced to admit to himself that the worst of his aches had disappeared and he was much more capable of sustaining long horseback journeys now. He was still subject to occasional stomach gripes and he was by no means as strong as he had once been, yet he was almost at the stage where he could enjoy the sights and smells and sounds around him for their own sake. He was amazed at how little sleep Katinka van Bak seemed to need. Half the time they rode on through the best part of the night before she was ready to make camp. As a result they made excellent time, but Hawkmoon felt permanently weary.

They reached the second main stage of their journey when they entered the territories of Duke Mikael of Bazhel, a distant kinsman of Hawkmoon's and for whom Katinka van Bak had once fought during the duke's squabble with another of his relatives, the now long-dead Pretender of Strasbourg. During the occupation of his lands by the Dark Empire, Duke Mikael had been subject to the grossest humiliation and he had never quite recovered from it. He had become distinctly misanthropic and his wife performed most of his functions for him. She was called Julia of Padova, daughter of the Traitor of Italia, Enric, who had formed a pact with the Dark Empire against his fellows and had been slain by the Beast Lords for his pains. Perhaps because of the knowledge she had of her father's baseness, Julia of Padova ruled the province well and with considerable fairness. Hawkmoon remarked on the wealth which was evident everywhere about the countryside. Fat cattle grazed on good grass. The farmhouses were well kept and shone with fresh paint and polished stone, their gables carved in the intricate style favoured by the peasants of these parts.

But when they came to Bazhel, the capital city, they

were received by Julia of Padova with only moderate politeness and her hospitality was not lavish. It seemed that she did not like to be reminded of the old, dark days when the Dark Empire had ruled the whole of Europe. Therefore she was not pleased to see Hawkmoon, for he had played such an important part against the Empire and thus she could not help but be reminded of it—of her husband's humiliation and of her father's treachery.

So it was that the pair did not remain long in Bazhel, but struck on for Munchenia, where the old Prince tried to smother them with gifts and begged them to stay longer and tell him of their adventures. Aside from warning him of what had happened in Ukrainia (he was sceptical) they told him nothing of their quest and reluctantly bade him farewell, armed with better weapons than those they had carried, and dressed in better clothes, though Hawkmoon had retained his big leather cloak, for the winter was making itself evident across the whole land now.

By the time Dorian Hawkmoon and Katinka van Bak reached Linz, now a Republic, the first snows had begun to fall in the streets of the little wooden city, rebuilt from that which had been completely razed by the armies of Granbretan.

'We must make better time,' Katinka van Bak told Hawkmoon as they sat in the tap-room of a good inn near the central square of the city. 'Else the passes in the Bulgar Mountains will be blocked to us and our whole journey will have no point.'

'I wonder if it does have point,' Hawkmoon said, sipping a negus with some relish, holding the steaming winecup in his gloved hands. He had now changed beyond recognition from the creature he had become at

Castle Brass, though all who had known him before
that time would have recognised him immediately. His
face had become strong again and muscles rippled beneath his silk shirt. His eyes were bright and healthy
and his skin glowed. His long fair hair shone.

'You wonder if you'll find Yisselda there?'

'That, aye. And I wonder if the army is as strong as
you thought. Perhaps they were lucky in the manner in
which they overwhelmed your forces.'

'Why do you think this now?'

'Because we have heard no rumours. Not a single hint
that anyone in these parts had received even an inkling
of this force which occupies the Bulgar Mountains.'

'I have seen this army,' Katinka van Bak reminded
him. 'And it is vast. Believe me in that. It is powerful.
It could take over the whole world. Believe me in
that also.'

Hawkmoon shrugged. 'Well, I do believe you, Katinka van Bak. But I still find it strange that no rumours
have come to our ears. When we have spoken of this
army there is never another who confirms what we
say. It is no wonder that little attention is paid to us!'

'Your brain sharpens,' said Katinka van Bak approv-
ingly, 'but as a result you are less able to believe the
fantastical!' She smiled. 'Is that not often the case?'

'Often, aye.'

'Would you turn back?'

Hawkmoon studied the hot wine in his cup. 'It is a
long journey home. But now I feel guilty, leaving my
duties in the Kamarg to go upon this quest.'

'You were not performing those duties very well,'
she reminded him softly. 'You were not in a position
to do so—mentally or physically.'

Hawkmoon smiled grimly. 'That's true. I have benefited a great deal from this journey. Yet that does not change the fact that my responsibilities lie firstly in the Kamarg.'

'It is a longer journey to the Kamarg, now, than it is to the Bulgar Mountains,' she said.

'You were at first reluctant to go on this quest,' he said. 'But now you are the most anxious of us to complete it!'

She shrugged. 'Say that I like to finish what I begin. Is that unusual?'

'I would say it was typical of you, Katinka van Bak.' Hawkmoon sighed. 'Very well. Let's go to the Bulgar Mountains, then, as quickly as our horses will take us. And let us make haste back to the Kamarg when our errand is done. With information and the strength of the Kamarg we shall find a way of defeating those who destroyed your land. We'll confer with Count Brass who, almost certainly, will have returned by then.'

'A sensible scheme, Hawkmoon.' Katinka van Bak seemed relieved. 'And now I'll to bed.'

'I'll finish my wine and copy your example,' said Hawkmoon. He laughed. 'You still manage to tire me out, even now.'

'Another month and our situation will be reversed,' she promised. 'Goodnight to you, Hawkmoon.'

Next morning their horses' hooves galloped through shallow snow and more snow was falling from an overcast sky. But by the early afternoon the clouds had cleared and the sky was blue and empty over their heads while the snow had begun to melt. It was not a serious fall, but it was an omen of what they might expect to find when they approached the Bulgar Mountains.

They rode through a hilly land which had once been part of the Kingdom of Wien, but so crushed had been that kingdom that its population had all but disappeared. Now grass had grown back on the burned ground and the many ruins were vine-covered and picturesque. Later travellers might come to marvel at such pretty relics, thought Hawkmoon, but he could never forget that they were the result of Granbretan's savage lust to rule the world.

They were passing the remains of a castle which looked down on them from a rise above the path they followed when Hawkmoon thought he heard a sound from the place.

He whispered to Katinka van Bak who was riding just ahead.

'Did you hear it? From the castle?'

'A human voice? Aye. I did. Could you hear the words?' She turned in her saddle to look back at him.

He shook his head. 'No. Should we investigate?'

'Our time runs short.' She pointed to the sky where more clouds were gathering.

But by now they had both pulled in their horses and were still, looking up at the castle.

'Good afternoon!'

The voice was strangely accented but cheerful.

'I had a feeling you would be passing this way, Champion.'

And from the ruins now stepped a slim young man wearing a hat with a huge brim, turned up at one side. There was a feather stuck in the band. He wore a velvet jerkin, rather dusty, and blue velvet pantaloons. On his feet were soft doeskin boots. He carried a small sack over his back. At his hip was a plain, slender sword.

And it was with horror that Dorian Hawkmoon recognised him.

Hawkmoon found himself drawing his sword, though the stranger had offered him no harm.

'What? You think me an enemy?' said the youth, smiling. 'I assure you that I am not.'

'You have seen him before, Hawkmoon?' Katinka van Bak said sharply. 'Who is he?'

He was the vision Hawkmoon had had when he lay upon his bed in Castle Brass, before the coming of the warrior woman.

'I know not,' said Hawkmoon thickly. 'This has a terrible smell of sorcery to it. Dark Empire work perhaps. He resembles—he looks like an old friend of mine —yet there is nothing evidently the same about them . . .'

'An old friend, eh?' said the stranger. 'Well I am that, Champion. What do they call you in this world?'

'I do not understand you.' Reluctantly Hawkmoon sheathed his sword.

'It is often the case when I recognise you. I am Jhary-a-Conel and I should not be here at all. But such strange disruptions have been taking place in the multiverse of late! I was wrenched from four separate incarnations in as many minutes! And what do they call you, then?'

'I still do not understand,' said Hawkmoon doggedly. 'Call me? I am the Duke von Köln. I am Dorian Hawkmoon.'

'Then greetings again, Duke Dorian. I am your companion. Though for how long I shall remain with you I know not. As I say, strange disruptions are . . .'

'You babble a considerable amount of nonsense, Sir Jhary,' said Katinka van Bak impatiently. 'How came you to these parts?'

'Through no volition of my own was I transported to this wasteland, madam.'

Suddenly the young man's bag began to jump and writhe and Jhary-a-Conel lowered it gently to the ground, opening it and drawing out a small, winged black and white cat. The same Hawkmoon had seen in the vision.

Hawkmoon shuddered. While he could find nothing to dislike about the young man himself, he had a terrible premonition that a-Conel's appearance heralded some unpleasant doom for him. Just as he could not see why he thought a-Conel resembled Oladahn, neither could he work out why other things were familiar, too. Echoes. Echoes like those which had convinced him Yisselda still lived . . .

'Do you know Yisselda?' he said tentatively. 'Yisselda of Brass?'

Jhary-a-Conel frowned. 'I do not believe so. But then I know so many people and forget most of them, just as I might well forget you some day. That is my fate. As, of course, it is yours.'

'You speak familiarly of my fate. Why should you know more of it than do I?'

'Because I do, in this context. Another time neither shall recognise the other. Champion, what calls you now?'

As a Champion of the Runestaff, Hawkmoon was used to this form of address, though it was rare for most to use it. The rest of the sentence was a mystery to him.

'Nothing calls me. I am upon a quest with this lady here. An urgent quest.'

'Then we must not delay. A moment.'

Jhary-a-Conel raced back up the hill and into the ruined castle. A moment later he emerged leading an old yellow horse. It was the unloveliest nag Hawkmoon had ever seen.

'I doubt if you would be able to keep up with us mounted on that creature,' Hawkmoon said. 'Even if we

had agreed that you should accompany us. And we
have not agreed.'

'But you will.' Jhary-a-Conel put a foot into a stirrup
and swung himself into his saddle. The horse seemed to
sag under his weight. 'After all, it is our fate to ride
together.'

'That may seem pre-ordained to you, my friend,' said
Hawkmoon grimly, 'but I share no such belief.' And
yet, he realised, he did. It seemed to him that it was
perfectly natural that Jhary should ride with them. At
the same time he resented both Jhary's assumption and
his own.

Hawkmoon looked to Katinka van Bak to see what
she thought. She merely shrugged. 'I've no objection
to another sword riding with us,' she said.

She cast a disdainful look at Jhary's horse. 'Not,'
she added, 'that I think you'll be riding with us for
long.'

'We shall see,' Jhary told her cheerfully. 'Where do
you ride?'

Hawkmoon became suspicious. Suddenly it occurred
to him that this man might be a spy for those who now
occupied the Bulgar Mountains.

'Why do you ask?'

Jhary shrugged. 'I wondered. I had heard of some
trouble in the mountains to the east of here. A wild
band who swoop down to destroy everything before
returning to their retreat.'

'I have heard a story like that,' Hawkmoon admitted
cautiously. 'Where did you hear it?'

'Oh, from a traveller I met on the road.'

At last Hawkmoon had heard confirmation of what
Katinka van Bak had told him. He was relieved to find
that she had not been lying to him. 'Well,' he said, 'we

ride in that general direction. Perhaps we shall see for ourselves.'

'Indeed,' said Katinka van Bak with a crooked smile.

And now there were three riding for the Bulgar Mountains. A strange threesome, in truth. They rode for some days and Jhary's nag appeared to have no great trouble in keeping pace with the other horses.

One day Hawkmoon turned to their new companion and asked him: 'Did you ever have occasion to meet a man called Oladahn? He was quite short and covered all over in red hair. He claimed to be kin to the Bulgar Mountain Giants (whom none, to my knowledge, has ever seen). An expert archer.'

'I've met many expert archers, among them Rackhir the Red Archer who is perhaps the greatest in all the multiverse, but never one called Oladahn. Was he a good friend of yours?'

'My closest friend for a long while.'

'Perhaps I have borne that name,' Jhary-a-Conel said frowning. 'I have borne many, of course. It seems vaguely familiar. Just as the name Corum or Urlik would seem familiar to you.'

'Urlik?' Hawkmoon felt the blood leave his face. 'What know you of that name?'

'It is your name. Or one of them, at least. As is Corum. Though Corum was not a human manifestation and would therefore be a little harder for you to recall.'

'You speak so casually of incarnations! Do you really mean to claim you can recall past lives as easily as I can recall past adventures?'

'Some lives. By no means all. And that is just as well. In another incarnation I might not remember this one, for instance. Yet my name has not changed, in this case, I note.'

Jhary laughed. 'My memories come and go. Just as yours do. It is what saves us.'

'You speak in riddles, friend Jhary.'

'So you often tell me.' Jhary shrugged. 'Yet this adventure does seem a little different, I'll admit. I am in the peculiar situation, at present, of being shifted willy-nilly through the dimensions at present. Disruptions on a large scale—brought about by the experiments of some foolish sorcerer, no doubt. And then, of course, there is always the interest that the Lords of Chaos show when such opportunities are offered. I would imagine they are playing some part in this.'

'The Lords of Chaos? Who are they?'

'Ah, it is something you must discover, if you do not know. Some say that they dwell at the end of time and their attempts to manipulate the universe according to their own desires are a result of their own world's dying. But that is a rather narrow theory. Others suggest that they do not exist at all, but are conjured up, periodically, by men's imaginations.'

'You are a sorcerer yourself, Master Jhary?' asked Katinka van Bak, falling back to join them.

'I think not.'

'A philosopher at least,' she said.

'My experience moulds my philosophy, that is all.'

And Jhary seemed to tire of the conversation and refused to be drawn further on that particular topic.

'My only experience of the sort you hint at,' said Hawkmoon, 'was with the Runestaff. Could the Runestaff be involved in what is happening in the Bulgar Mountains?'

'The Runestaff? Perhaps.'

* * *

Snow had fallen heavily on the great city of Pesht. Built of white, carved stone, the city had survived the Dark Empire sieges and now looked much as it had done before Granbretan had ridden out on her conquerings. Snow sparkled on every surface and its glare, as they approached at night under a full moon, made it seem that Pesht burned with white fire.

They arrived at the gates after midnight and had some difficulty rousing the guard who let them in with a considerable amount of grumbling and querying their business in the city. Down broad, deserted avenues they rode, seeking the palace of Prince Karl of Pesht. Prince Karl had once courted Katinka van Bak and asked her to be his wife. They had been lovers for three years, the warrior woman had told Hawkmoon, but she would never marry him. Now he had married a princess from Zagredia and was happy. They were friends. She had stayed with him during her flight from Ukrainia. He would be surprised to see her.

Prince Karl of Pesht was surprised. He arrived in his own ornate hall in a brocade dressing gown, his eyes still thick with sleep. But he was pleased to see Katinka van Bak.

'Katinka! I thought you planned to winter in the Kamarg!'

'That had been my plan.' She went forward and seized the tall old man's shoulders, kissing him swiftly on both cheeks in the military fashion, so that it seemed more as if she was presenting a soldier with a medal than greeting an ex-lover. 'But Duke Dorian here persuaded me to accompany him to the Bulgar Mountains.'

'Dorian? The Duke of Köln. I have heard much of you, young man. It is an honour to have you under my roof.' Prince Karl smiled as he shook Hawkmoon's hand. 'And this?'

'A companion of the road,' said Hawkmoon. 'His name is a strange one. Jhary-a-Conel.'

Jhary swept off his hat in an elaborate bow. 'An honour to meet the Prince of Pesht,' he said.

Prince Karl laughed. 'A privilege to entertain any companion of the great Hero of Londra. This is wonderful. You will stay for some time?'

'For the night only, I regret,' said Hawkmoon. 'Our business in the Bulgar Mountains is urgent.'

'What could possibly take you there? Even the legendary mountain giants are all dead now, I gather.'

'You have not told the prince?' said Hawkmoon in surprise, turning to Katinka van Bak. 'Of the raiders. I thought . . .'

'I did not wish to alarm him,' she said.

'But his city is not so distant from the Bulgar Mountains that it cannot be in danger of attack!' Hawkmoon said.

'Attack? What is this? An enemy from beyond the mountains?' Prince Karl's expression changed.

'Bandits,' said Katinka van Bak, darting a hard, meaning glance at Hawkmoon. 'A city of the size of Pesht has nothing to fear. A land so well defended as yours is under no threat.'

'But . . .' Hawkmoon restrained himself. Plainly Katinka van Bak had a reason for not telling the Prince of Pesht all she knew. But what could that reason possibly be? Did she suspect Prince Karl of being in league with her enemies? If so, she could have warned him earlier. Besides, it was inconceivable that this fine old man would ally him with such a rabble. He had fought well and nobly against the Dark Empire and had been imprisoned for his pains, though he had not been subjected to the indignities normally visited upon captured enemy aristocrats by the Dark Empire.

'You will be weary from so much riding,' said Prince
Karl tactfully. He had already ordered his servants to
prepare rooms for his guests. 'You will want to seek
your beds. I have been selfish in thinking only of my
own pleasure at seeing you again, Katinka, and meeting
this hero here.' He smiled and put his arm around
Hawkmoon's shoulders. 'But at breakfast, perhaps, we
can talk a little. Before you leave?'

'It would please me greatly, sire,' said Hawkmoon.

And when Hawkmoon lay in a great bed in a well-
appointed room in which a comfortable fire blazed, he
watched the shadows playing on the rich tapestries
which decorated the walls and he brooded for a few
minutes on the reasons for Katinka van Bak's reticence
before falling into a deep and dreamless sleep.

The big sleigh could have taken a dozen armoured
men and could have been sold for a fortune, for it was
inlaid with gold, platinum, ivory and ebony, as well as
precious jewels. The carvings cut into the wood of its
frame were the work of a master. Hawkmoon and
Katinka van Bak had been reluctant to accept the gift
from Prince Karl, but he was insistent. 'It is what you
will need in this weather. Your riding beasts can follow
and thus be fresh when you need them.' Eight black
geldings pulled the sleigh and they were clad in harness
of black leather and fine silver. Silver bells had been
fixed to the harness, but these had been muffled for
obvious reasons.

The snow was falling thickly and the roads which led
to Pesht were all slippery with ice. It was logical to use
a sleigh under such circumstances. The sleigh was piled
with provisions, with furs, with a pavilion which could
be quickly erected in even the worst weather. There
were ancient devices, relatives to the flame-lances, on

which food could be prepared. And there seemed enough food of all kinds to feed a small army. Prince Karl had not been expressing mere politeness when he had said he was delighted to receive them.

Jhary-a-Conel felt no reluctance in accepting the sleigh. He laughed with pleasure as he climbed in and seated himself amidst a profusion of expensive furs. 'Remember when you were Urlik,' he said, addressing Hawkmoon, 'Urlik Skarsol, Prince of the Southern Ice. Bears drew your carriage then!'

'I remember no such experience,' said Hawkmoon sharply. 'I wish I could understand your motives in continuing this pretence.'

'Ah, well,' replied Jhary philosophically, 'perhaps you will understand later.'

Prince Karl of Pesht bid them farewell personally, waving to them from Pesht's impressive walls until they were out of sight.

The great sleigh moved swiftly and Hawkmoon wondered why the speed of its travelling filled him with a mixture of exhilaration and misgivings. Again Jhary had mentioned something which roused an echo of memory. And yet it was obvious to him that he could never have been this 'Urlik'—for all he seemed to remember dreaming once of such a name.

And now the going was speedy, for the weather had been turned to their advantage. The eight black geldings seemed tireless as they strained in their harness, dragging the sleigh closer and closer to the Bulgar Mountains.

But still Hawkmoon had a terrifying sense of familiarity. The image of a silver chariot, its four wheels fixed to skis, moving implacably over a great ice plain. Another image of a ship—but a ship which travelled upon another ice plain. And they were not the same worlds—of that he was sure. Neither was either one this world, his world. He drove the thoughts away as best he could, but they were persistent.

Perhaps he should put all his questions to Katinka van Bak and to Jhary-a-Conel, but he could not bring himself to ask them. He felt that the answers might not be to his taste.

So they drove on through the swirling snow and the ground rose steeply and the speed of their travelling decreased a little, but not very much.

From what he could see of the surrounding landscape, there was no evidence at all of recent raids. Sitting with his hands on the reins of the eight black geldings, Hawkmoon put this to Katinka van Bak.

Her answer was brief:

'Why should there be such signs? I told you that they raided only on the other side of the mountains.'

'Then there must be an explanation for that,' Hawkmoon said. 'And if we find the explanation we might also find their weakness.'

Finally the roads became too steep and the geldings' hooves slipped on the ice as they strove to haul the sleigh behind them. The snow had abated and it was late in the afternoon. Hawkmoon pointed to a mountain meadow below them. 'The horses may be pastured there. The grazing is reasonable and—look—a cave where they might stable themselves. It is the most we can do for them, I fear.'

'Very well,' agreed Katinka van Bak. With great difficulty they managed to turn the horses and lead them back down the path until they reached the snow-covered meadow. Hawkmoon cleared snow with his boot to indicate the grass below, but the geldings needed no help from him. They were used to such conditions and were soon using their hooves to clear the snow so that they

might graze. And since it was almost sunset, the three
decided to spend the night in the cave with the horses
before continuing into the mountains.

'These conditions are an advantage,' said Hawkmoon. 'For our enemies have little chance of seeing us.'

'True enough,' said Katinka van Bak.

'And similarly,' Hawkmoon went on, 'we must be
wary. For we shall not see them until they are upon
us. Do you know this area, Katinka van Bak?'

'I know it fairly well,' she told him. She was lighting
a fire inside the cave for their cooking stoves, provided
by the prince, did not give out enough heat to warm the
cave.

'This is snug,' said Jhary-a-Conel. 'I would not mind
spending the rest of the winter here. Then we could
travel on when spring comes.'

Katinka offered him a glance of contempt. He grinned
and kept silence for a while.

They led their horses now, beneath a cold, hard sky.
Save for a little withered moss and some stunted grey
and brown birches, nothing grew in these mountains. A
sharp wind blew. A few carrion birds wheeled away
amongst the jagged peaks. The sounds of their breathing, of their horses' hooves clicking on the rocks, of
their own slippery progress, were the only sounds. The
scenery viewed from these high mountain paths was
beautiful in the extreme, yet it was also deadly. It was
dead. It was cold. It was cruel. Many travellers must
have died in these parts during the season of winter.

Hawkmoon wore a thick fur robe over his leather
coat. Though he sweated, he did not dare take any of
his clothing off for fear he would freeze to the spot when
he stopped. The others, too, wore heavy furs—hoods,
gloves and boots as well as coats. And the climbing was

almost always upward. Only occasionally might a path take a downward turn, only to soar again around the next bend.

Yet the mountains, for all their deadly beauty, seemed peaceful. An immense sense of peace filled the valleys, and Hawkmoon could barely believe that a great force of bandits hid here. There was no atmosphere to indicate that the mountains had been invaded. He felt as if he were one of the first human beings ever to come this way. Although the going was difficult and very wearying, he felt more relaxed here than he had felt since he had been a child in Köln, when the old Duke, his father, had ruled. His responsibilities had become simple. To stay alive.

And at last they reached a slightly wider path where there was room enough for Hawkmoon to stretch to his full length had he so desired. And this path ended suddenly at a big, black cave entrance.

'What's this?' Hawkmoon asked Katinka. 'It seems a dead end. Is it a tunnel?'

'Aye,' replied Katinka van Bak. 'It's a tunnel.'

'And how much further do we journey when we reach the other end of the tunnel?'

Hawkmoon leaned against the rock wall, just at the entrance to the tunnel.

'That depends,' said Katinka van Bak mysteriously. And she would not say more.

Hawkmoon was too weary to ask her what she meant. Jerking his body forward, he plunged into the tunnel, leading his horse behind him, glad that snow no longer dragged at his boots once he had gone a few yards into the great cavern. Inside it was quite warm and there was a smell. It was almost like the smell of spring. Hawkmoon remarked on it, but neither of the others could smell the odour so that he wondered if perhaps

some perfume clung to his big fur cloak. The floor
of the cavern levelled out now and it became much
easier to walk. 'It is hard to believe,' said Hawkmoon,
'that this place is natural. It is a wonder of the world.'

They had been walking for an hour, with no sight of
the other end of the tunnel, when Hawkmoon began to
feel nervous.

'It cannot be natural,' he repeated. He ran his gloved
hands along the walls, but there were no signs of tools
having been used to create them. He turned back to the
others and thought, in the gloom, that he noticed peculiar expressions on both their faces. 'What do you
think? You know this place, Katinka van Bak. Are there
any mentions of it in the histories? In legends?'

'Some,' she admitted. 'Go on, Hawkmoon. We shall
soon be at the other side.'

'But where does it lead?' He brought his body fully
round to confront them. The fireglobe in his hand
burned dully and turned his face to a demonic red. 'Directly to the Dark Empire camp? Do you two work for
my old enemies? Is this a ruse? You have neither of
you told me enough!'

'We are not in the pay of your enemies,' said Katinka van Bak. 'Continue, Hawkmoon, please. Or shall
I lead?' She stepped forward.

Hawkmoon involuntarily put a hand to the hilt of
his sword, pushing back his great fur cloak to do so.
'No. I trust you, Katinka van Bak, yet everything in me
warns me of a trap. How can this be?'

'You must go on, Sir Champion!' said Jhary-a-Conel
quietly, stroking the fur of his small black and white
cat, which had emerged from his jerkin. 'You must.'

'Champion? Champion of what?' Still Hawkmoon's
hand gripped the sword hilt. 'Of what?'

'Champion Eternal,' said Jhary-a-Conel, softly still. 'Fate's soldier . . .'

'No!' Though the words were all but meaningless, Hawkmoon could not bear to hear them. 'No!!'

His gloved hands flew to his ears.

And that was when his two friends rushed at him.

He was still not as strong as he had been before his madness. He was weary from the climb. He struggled against them until he felt Katinka van Bak's dagger pricking his eye and he heard her urgent voice in his ear:

'Killing you is the easiest way to achieve our purpose, Hawkmoon,' she said. 'But it would not be the kindest. Besides, I am reluctant to cut you off from this body, should you desire to return to it. Thus I shall only kill you if you make it impossible for me to do ought else. Do you understand?'

'I understand treachery,' he said savagely, still testing his strength against their clutches, 'and I thought I smelled the spring. I smelled traitors, instead. Traitors who posed as friends.'

One of them extinguished the fireglobe. The three stood in blackness and Hawkmoon heard the echoes of his words.

'Where is this place?' He felt the dagger point prick his eye again. 'What are you doing to me?'

'It was the only way,' said Katinka van Bak. 'It was the only way, Champion.'

It was the first time she had called him that, though Jhary had used the term frequently.

'Where is this place?' he said again. 'Where?'

'I wish that I knew,' said Katinka van Bak. And her voice was almost sad.

Then she evidently struck him on the back of the

head with her armoured gauntlet. He felt the blow and
guessed what caused it. For a moment he thought that
it had not succeeded in its intention of driving con-
sciousness from him. Then he realised that he had sunk
to his knees.

Then he realised that his body seemed to be falling
away from him in the blackness of the cave.

And then he knew that her blow had done what it
had intended, after all.

BOOK TWO

A HOMECOMING

CHAPTER ONE

ILIAN OF GARATHORM

Hawkmoon listened to ghosts.

Each ghost spoke to him in his own voice.

In Hawkmoon's voice . . .

. . . then I was Erekosë and I slew the human race. And Urlik Skarsol, Prince of the Southern Ice, who slew the Silver Queen from Moon. Who bore the Black Sword. Now I hang in limbo and await my next task. Perhaps through this I shall find a means of returning to my lost love Ermizhad. Perhaps I shall find Tanelorn.

(I have been Elric)

Fate's soldier . . . Time's tool . . . Champion Eternal . . . Doomed to perpetual strife.

(I have been Corum. In more than one life I have been Corum)

I know not how it began. Perhaps it will end in Tanelorn.

Rhalina, Yisselda, Cymoril, Zarozina . . .

So many women.

(I have been Arflane. Asquiol. Aubec.)

All die, save me.

(I have been Hawkmoon . . .)

'No! I am Hawkmoon!'

(We are all Hawkmoon. Hawkmoon is all of us)

All live, save me.

John Daker? Was he the first?

Or the last?

I have betrayed so many and been betrayed so much.

Faces floated before him. Each face was different. Each face was his own face. He shouted and tried to push them away.

But he had no hands.

He tried to revive himself. Better to die under Katinka van Bak's knife than suffer this torment. It was what he had feared. It was what he had tried to avoid. It was the reason he had not pursued his argument with Jhary-a-Conel. But he was alone against a thousand—a thousand manifestations of himself.

The struggle is eternal. The fight is endless.

And now we must become Ilian. Ilian, whose soul was driven out. Is this not a strange task?

'*I am Hawkmoon. Only Hawkmoon.*'

And I am Hawkmoon. And I am Urlik Skarsol. And I am Ilian of Garathorm. Perhaps here I shall find Tanelorn. Farewell to the South Ice and the dying sun. Farewell to the Silver Queen and the Screaming Chalice. Farewell Count Brass. Farewell Urlik. Farewell Hawkmoon . . .

And Hawkmoon began to feel his memories fading from him. In their place came crowding a million other memories. Memories of bizarre worlds and exotic landscapes, of creatures both human and inhuman. Memories that could not possibly belong to a single man, and yet they were like those dreams he had had at Castle Brass. Or had he experienced them at Castle Brass? Perhaps it had been elsewhere? In Melniboné? In Loos Ptokai? In Castle Erorn by the sea? Aboard that strange ship which travelled beyond the Earth? Where? Where had he dreamed those dreams?

And he knew that he had dreamed them in all of

those places and that he would dream them again in all those places.

He knew that there was no such thing as Time.

Past, present and future were all the same. They existed all at the same moment—and they did not exist at any moment.

He was Urlik Skarsol, Prince of the Southern Ice, and his chariot was drawn by bears, moving across the ice beneath a dying sun. Moving towards a goal. Searching, as Hawkmoon searched for Yisselda, for a woman whom he could not reach. Ermizhad. And Ermizhad had not loved Urlik Skarsol. She had loved Erekosë. Yet Erekosë was Urlik Skarsol, too.

Tanelorn. That was Urlik's goal.

Tanelorn. Should it be Hawkmoon's?

The name was so familiar. Yet he had found Tanelorn many times. He had dwelled there once and each time Tanelorn had been different.

Which Tanelorn must he seek?

And there was a sword. A sword which had many manifestations. A black sword. Yet it was often disguised. A sword . . .

Ilian of Garathorm bore a good sword. Ilian felt for it, but it was not there. Ilian's hands ran over chain mail, over silk, over flesh. Ilian's hands touched cool turf and Ilian's nose smelled the richness of spring. Ilian's eyes opened. Two strangers stood there, a young man and a middle-aged woman. Yet their faces were familiar.

Hawkmoon said: 'Katinka van . . .' and then Ilian forgot the rest of the name. Hawkmoon felt his body and was astonished. 'What have you made me into . . .?' And Ilian wondered at those words, even though they came from Ilian's mouth.

'Greetings, Ilian of Garathorm, Champion Eternal,' said the young man with a smile. He had a small black and white cat on his shoulder. The cat had a pair of wings folded on its back.

'And Hawkmoon, farewell—for the moment, at least,' said the middle-aged woman who was dressed all in battered plate armour.

Ilian said vaguely: 'Hawkmoon? The name is familiar. Yet I thought for an instant I was called Urlik Skarsol, also. Who are you?'

The young man bowed, showing none of the patronising mockery or condescension with which Ilian had become familiar, even when at court.

'I am Jhary-a-Conel. And this lady is Katinka van Bak, whom you may remember.'

Ilian frowned. 'Yes . . . Katinka van Bak. You are the one who saved me when Ymryl's pack pursued me . . .'

And then, for a moment, Ilian's memory faded.

Hawkmoon said, through Ilian's lips: 'What have you done to me, Katinka van Bak?' He felt at his body in horror. His skin was softer. His form was different. He had become shorter. 'You have made me into . . . into a woman!'

Jhary-a-Conel leaned forward, his eyes full of an abnormal intensity. 'It had to be done. You are Ilian of Garathorm. This world needs Ilian. Trust us. It will benefit Hawkmoon, too.'

'You plotted this together. There was no army in the Bulgar Mountains! That tunnel . . .'

'It led here. To Garathorm,' Katinka van Bak said. 'I discovered this passage between the dimensions when I hid from the Dark Empire. I was here when Ymryl and the others arrived. I saved your life, Ilian, but they were able, with their sorcery, to drive your spirit from you. I was in despair for Garathorm. Then I met Jhary here. He conceived a solution. Hawkmoon was close to the point of death. As a manifestation of the eternal Champion his spirit could substitute for Ilian's—for she is another manifestation of that Champion, you see. That story I told you. I knew it might bring you here— through the tunnel. The army I described does raid beyond the Bulgar Mountains. It raids Garathorm.'

Hawkmoon's brain was whirling. 'I don't understand. I occupy another's body? Is that what you are saying? This *can* only be Dark Empire work!'

'Believe us that it is not!' said Katinka van Bak seriously.

'Though the Dark Empire has played some part, I feel, in bringing this disaster about,' said Jhary-a-Conel. 'The exact part is yet to be discovered. But only as Ilian can you hope to oppose those who now rule this world. It is Ilian's fate, you see. Only Ilian's. Hawkmoon could not have succeeded . . .'

'So you have imprisoned me in this woman's body . . . But how? What sorcery accomplished it?'

Jhary looked at the grassy ground. 'I have some skill in this particular area. But you must forget that you are Hawkmoon. Hawkmoon has no place in Garathorm. You *must* be Ilian, or our work is wasted. Ilian—whom Ymryl desired. And because he could not possess her, he drove her spirit from her. Even Ymryl did not realise what he was doing—that Ilian's destiny is to wage war against him. Ymryl merely sees you, Ilian, as a desirable woman, albeit a fierce foe who led the remnants of her father's army against him.'

'Ymryl . . .' Hawkmoon strove to hang on to his own identity, but it was slipping away from him again. 'Ymryl, who serves Chaos. Ymryl, the Yellow Horn. They came from nowhere and Garathorm fell to them. Ah, I remember the fires. I remember my father, kindly

Pyran. With all his reluctance to fight, he battled Ymryl long . . .'

'And then you took up Pyran's flaming banner. Remember, Ilian? You took up that burning flag, the fame of all Garathorm, and you rode against Ymryl's force . . .' Katinka van Bak said softly. 'I had taught you the use of sword, shield and axe, while I guested at Pyran's court, after I fled the Dark Empire. And you put all my learning to splendid use until only you and I remained alive upon the field.'

'I remember,' said Ilian. 'And we were only spared because they were amused to discover our feminine sex. Ah, the humiliation I felt when Ymryl tugged the helm from my head! "You shall rule beside me," he said. And he reached out a hand still covered in the blood of my people, and he touched my body! Oh, I remember.' Ilian's voice became hard and fierce. 'And I remember that it was then I swore to slay him. Yet there was only one way and I was unable to follow it. I could not. And, because I resisted him, he imprisoned me . . .'

'Which was when I was able to rescue you. We fled. His pack followed. We fought it and destroyed it. But Ymryl's sorcerers found us. In his rage he made them reach out and drive your spirit from you.'

'Ah, the sending. Yes. They attacked. I remember nothing more.'

'We were hiding in the cave. I had some idea to take you through, back to my own world where I thought you would be safe. But then, when your soul went out of you, there was no point to it. I met Jhary-a-Conel, who had been drawn to Garathorm by the same forces which brought Ymryl. Between us we determined what we must try to do. Your memories were still within your skull. Only an—an *essence*—was lacking. So we had to find a new soul. And Hawkmoon's was not in use then, as he rotted in his tower at Castle Brass. With many misgivings we did what we had to do. And now you have a soul again.'

'And Ymryl?'

'He believes you—gone. He has doubtless forgotten you and thinks he rules all Garathorm with nothing to fear. His rabble army rides roughshod over all the land. Yet even those creatures have hardly been able to spoil Garathorm's beauty.'

'Garathorm is still lovely,' agreed Ilian. She looked from where she stood on the slopes of the hill, the cave mouth behind her, and saw her world with fresh eyes, as if for the first time.

Not far off was the edge of the great forest—the forest which covered this world's single continent. Save for Garathorm, all the rest was sea containing the occasional small island. And the trees were huge. Some stretched several hundred feet into the air.

The sky was wide and blue and in it burned a huge golden sun. The sun shone on flowers whose heads measured more than twelve feet across. It made their colours almost blinding in their intensity. Scarlets, purples and yellows predominated. Among the blooms flew butterflies whose proportions matched those of the flowers and whose colours were even richer. One particularly glorious insect had wings measuring nearly two feet long. And among the vine-hung boles of the trees fluttered great birds, their plumage glittering in the deep shadows of the forest. And Ilian knew that there was hardly a bird or a beast in that forest which a human had to fear. She breathed the thick air with relish and she smiled.

'Yes,' she said, 'I am Ilian of Garathorm. Who

could wish to be anything else? Who would want to dwell anywhere but in Garathorm, even in these times?'

'Exactly,' said Jhary-a-Conel in some relief.

Katinka van Bak began to unwrap a big fur cloak which Ilian did not recall having seen before. In the cloak was a variety of stone pots. The lids of the pots were sealed with wax.

'Preserves,' explained Katinka van Bak. 'Meats, fruits and vegetables. These will sustain us for a while. Let's eat now.'

And while they ate, Ilian recalled the terrors of the past months.

Garathorm had become a united land some two centuries earlier, thanks to the diplomacy (not to mention the lust for power) of Ilian's ancestors. And for those two hundred years there had been peace and prosperity for all the inhabitants of the great arboreal continent. Learning flourished, as did the arts. Garathorm's capital, the ebony city of Virinthorm, had grown to great proportions. Its suburbs stretched for several miles from the old city, under the branches of the great, sheltering trees, which protected Garathorm from the heavy rains which, for a month every year, beat down upon the island continent. Once, it was said, there had been other continents and Garathorm had been a desert. Then some cataclysm had swept the earth, perhaps causing the melting of the polar ice, and when the cataclysm was past, only Garathorm remained. And Garathorm was changed, becoming a place where foliage grew to enormous proportions. The reason for this was still unknown. Garathorm's scholars had yet to find a clue to the answer. Perhaps it lay beneath the sea, in the drowned lands.

Twenty years earlier Ilian's father, Pyran, had come

to the throne on the death of his uncle. Ilian had been born but two years before, almost to the day. And Pyran's rule began what many believed to be a Golden Age for Garathorm. Ilian had grown up in an atmosphere of humanity and happiness. Always an active girl, she had spent much time riding the ostrich-like *vayna* through the forests. The *vayna* could make considerable speed upon the ground, and almost as good speed when it ran along the thick branches of the trees, leaping from branch to branch with a rider clinging to its back. It was one of the most exhilarating pastimes in Garathorm. And when, several years ago, Katinka van Bak had suddenly arrived at the court of King Pyran, exhausted, confused and close to death from many wounds, Ilian took to her immediately. Katinka's story had been a strange one. Somehow she had been transported through time—either into the future or the past, she could not be sure—after fleeing from enemies who had defeated her in a great battle. The details of her passage through time were vague, but she had soon become a welcome guest at the court and, to occupy her own mind as much as to help Ilian, had agreed to teach Ilian the martial arts. In Garathorm there were no warriors. There was only a ceremonial guard and groups of others who task it was to protect the remoter farmsteads against attacks from the few wild beasts which still remained in Garathorm. Yet Ilian took to the sword and the axe as if she was the cub of some ancient reaver. It was as if she had always pursued such arts. And she found a peculiar satisfaction in learning everything Katinka van Bak could teach her. For all that her childhood had been happy, it had always seemed to lack something until that moment.

Her father had been amused by her enthusiasm for such archaic pursuits. And her enthusiasm had been in-

fectious amongst many of the young people at court.
Eventually there had been several hundred girls and
boys who felt at ease with a sword and a buckler and
elaborate mock tournaments became a feature of court
festivals.

Perhaps it was not coincidence, then, but some working of Fate, that had prepared a small but highly skilled
army to resist Ymryl when he came.

Ymryl had come suddenly to Virinthorm. A few
rumours had arrived ahead of him and King Pyran had
sent emissaries to investigate the disturbing reports
coming from the remoter quarters of the continent. But
before the emissaries could return, Ymryl had arrived.
It emerged later that he was part of a larger army
which had swept over the whole of Garathorm and
taken all the main provincial cities within a matter of
weeks. At first it was thought that they had come from
some previously unknown land beyond the sea, but
there was no evidence to suggest it. Like Katinka van
Bak, Ymryl and his comrades had arrived mysteriously in Garathorm. They hardly seemed, themselves, to
know how they had got here.

Speculation as to their origin became unimportant.
All efforts were put into resisting them. Scholars were
asked to invent weapons. Engineers, too, found that
they were asked to put their skills to conceiving methods
of destruction. They were not used to thinking in such
terms and few weapons were produced. Katinka van
Bak, Ilian and about two hundred others, harried
Ymryl's rabble army, and scored a few victories in
skirmishes, but when Ymryl was ready to march against
the tree-sheltered city of Virinthorm, he marched. He
could not be resisted. There were two battles fought in
the great glade beyond the city. At the first battle King
Pyran brought out the ancient war-flag of his ancestors

—the burning flag, which blazed with a strange fire and which was made of a cloth which never perished. With that flag held in his own hand, he went against Ymryl, leading an army of poorly armed and untrained citizens. King Pyran was slaughtered with his folk and Ilian had barely managed to drag the burning banner from his dead hand before she escaped with the remains of her own professional fighters—those who had once shared her enthusiasm for military arts and who had swiftly become hardened veterans.

There had been one last battle in which Ilian and Katinka van Bak had led a few hundred survivors aganist Ymryl. They had put up a splendid fight and taken many of the invaders that day, but they were eventually beaten. Ilian was not sure if any of her people had escaped, but there seemed to be no survivors, save herself and Katinka van Bak.

And they had been captured. And Ymryl had lusted for her and seen, too, that with her at his side he would have no difficulty in ruling those citizens who still hid in the forests beyond Virinthorm and crept out at night to slaughter his men.

When she had resisted him, he had given orders that she should be imprisoned, that she should be kept awake and fed only the minimum to keep her alive. He had known that she would eventually agree to what he wanted.

And now, as she ate, Ilian suddenly remembered what she had done. Something which Katinka van Bak had not mentioned. And Ilian could barely swallow the food in her mouth as she turned to look at Katinka van Bak.

'Why did you not remind me of that?' she said coldly. 'Of my brother.'

'You were not to blame for that,' said Katinka van

Bak. The older woman lowered her eyes to the ground.
'I should have done what you did. Anyone would. They
tortured you.'

'And I told them. I told them where he would be
hiding. And they found him and they slew him.'

'They tortured you,' said Katinka van Bak harshly.
'They tore your body. They abused it. They did not let
you sleep. They did not let you eat. They wanted two
things from you. You only gave them one. That was a
triumph!'

'You mean I gave them my brother instead of myself.
Is that a triumph?'

'In the circumstances, yes. Forget it, Ilian. We may
yet avenge your brother—and the rest.'

'I must do much to atone for that thing,' said Ilian.
She knew there were tears in her eyes and she tried to
force them back.

'There is much, anyway, that must be done,' said
Jhary-a-Conel.

CHAPTER TWO

OUTLAWS OF A THOUSAND SPHERES

The small black and white cat drifted high above the forest on a warm upcurrent of air. The sun was setting. The cat waited, for it preferred to go about its business at night. From the ground, if it could be seen at all, the cat would have been mistaken for a hawk. It hovered, keeping its position by the slightest movements of its wings, close to a city but recently occupied by a huge and ferocious army.

Katinka van Bak had not lied when she had described the army which had defeated her. Her only lie concerned where she had engaged this army and what its intentions were. In a sense, of course, it had occupied the Bulgar Mountains, for did not this land, in some mysterious way, exist within that range?

As the sun sank, so the small black and white cat dropped lower and lower until at last it had settled upon a branch close to the top of one of the tallest trees. A breeze blew, rustling the leaves and making the trees, from where the cat sat, seem to move like the waves of a strange sea.

The cat jumped and landed on a lower branch, jumped again and this time spread its wings, soaring a few feet before finding another foothold.

Slowly it began to descend towards the city, whose lights could be seen far below. Not for the first time was the cat scouting for its master, Jhary-a-Conel; going somewhere where Jhary himself, or his friends, could not go.

At last the cat lay stretched on a branch directly over the centre of the city. Virinthorm had no walls, for it had been long since she had needed them, and all her main buildings were built of carved, polished ebony, inlaid with whale ivory bought from the coastal peoples to the south. Those people had once hunted whales, but now the few who were left were hunted by monsters themselves. The other buildings were all built of hard-wood, for stone was a rarity in Garathorm, and all had a rich, mellow look to them—those which had been left untouched by the invaders' brands.

The cat dropped still lower, digging its claws into the smooth roof of a large building and climbing to the main beam.

A terrible smell filled the city. It was a smell of death and of decay. The cat found it at once unpleasant and interesting, but it denied itself the instinct to explore the source of the odours. Instead it spread its wings and flew away from the building and then back again, losing height rapidly and then gliding gracefully through an open window.

The cat's unusual sixth sense had not betrayed it. It found itself in a bedroom. The room was strewn with rich brocades, silks and feather cloaks. The bed was unmade and in great disorder. Empty wine-cups were scattered everywhere and there was evidence that much wine had been spilled throughout the room over the course of weeks or months. On the bed lay a naked man. To one side of him, huddled in each other's arms and sleeping fitfully, lay two young girls. There were many minor cuts and bruises on their bodies. Both had black hair and pale skins. The man had bright yellow hair, which might have been dyed. The hair on his body was not the same colour, but a reddish brown. It was an extremely muscular body and it must have measured at least seven feet long. The head was large and tapered from the wide cheek-bones to the jaw, almost to a point. It was a brutish head and a powerful head, yet there was also a look of weakness in it. Something about that pointed jaw and that cruel mouth made the face not quite handsome (though some might have found it so) and instead it was oddly repulsive.

This was Ymryl.

Around his thick neck was slung by a cord a silver-dressed amber horn.

This was Ymryl, the Yellow Horn.

And his horn could be heard for miles, if he needed to summon his men. And it was said that the notes of that horn could be heard elsewhere, too. It was said that they could be heard in Hell, where Ymryl had comrades.

Ymryl stirred, as if he sensed the cat's presence. The cat swiftly flew to a ledge high up on the far wall. Trophies had once been kept there, but the gold shield, won by one of Ilian's ancestors, had been dragged from its place months before. Ymryl coughed and groaned and opened his eyes a fraction. He rolled over on the bed and leaning his elbows on the back of one of the girls poured himself wine from the jug which rested on the nearby table. He drained the wine-cup, sniffed and sat up straighter on the bed.

'Garko!' growled Ymryl. 'Garko! Here!'

From another room a creature came scuttling. The creature had four short legs, a round torso into which was set a face, and long spindly arms ending in large hands.

'Master?' whispered Garko.

'What's the hour?'

'Just past sunset, master.'

'So I've slept through the day, have I?' Ymryl got up and dragged on a dirty robe, looted from the king's own chests. 'Doubtless it has been another dull day. No news from the west?'

'None. If they planned to attack, we should know by now, lord.'

'I suppose so. By Arioch! I grow bored, Garko. I begin to suspect that somehow we are all in this damned place as a punishment. I wish I knew how I had offended the Lords of Chaos, if that's the case. We thought at first that we had been given a paradise to loot. Few of the people knew the first thing about making war. It was so easy to take over their cities. And now we find ourselves with nothing to do. How go the sorcerer's experiments?'

'He remains frustrated in his attempts to get his dimension travelling machine to work for him. I have little faith in him, master.'

Ymryl sniffed. 'Well, he slew the maid for me—or the next best thing. And at some distance. That was clever. Perhaps he will yet find a way through for us.'

'Perhaps, master.'

'I cannot understand why even the most powerful amongst us is unable to summon word from the Lords of Chaos. If I were not Ymryl, the Yellow Horn, if I were a lesser man, I should feel abandoned. I ruled a great nation in my own world, Garko. I ruled it in the name of Chaos. I gave Arioch many sacrifices, Garko. Many.'

'So you have told me, master.'

'And there are others here who were kings in their own worlds. Some ruled empires. And barely one of us seems to have shared the same time or even the same plane. That is what puzzles me. Each creature—human or unhuman (like yourself)—came here at the identical moment, and came here from a different world. It could only be the work of Arioch. Or some other powerful Chaos Lord, for we are all—or most of us—servants of those great Lords of Entropy. And still Arioch does not tell us his reason for bringing us here.'

'It could be that he has none, master.'

Ymryl snorted. Without much anger, he cuffed Garko across the top of his head. 'Arioch always has reasons. Yet he is good to those who serve him without question—as I served him for many years in my own world. I thought at first that this must be a reward . . .'

Ymryl took his jug and his cup to the window and stared out at the city he had conquered while he poured himself more wine. He tilted back his yellow head and gulped the wine. 'I grow so bored. So bored. I thought those who took the westerly provinces would have become greedy by now and would have tried to attack us. But they, it seems, are as wary as I. They do not wish to anger Arioch by turning on the others. I am beginning to alter my thinking on that subject now. I think Arioch expects us to fight. He wishes to discover which is the strongest. That could be why we were brought here. A test, you see, Garko.'

'A test. I see, master.'

Ymryl sniffed. 'Summon the sorcerer. I would consult with him. It could be that he can help me understand what to do.'

Garko backed from the room. 'I will summon him, master.'

The small black and white cat watched as Ymryl strode about the room, his brows drawn in thought. There was an immense sense of physical power about the man and yet at the same time there was an indecisiveness which perhaps he had not always had. Perhaps, before he pledged himself to Chaos, he had been stronger. It was often said that Chaos warped those who served it—and not always physically.

Once Ymryl paused and stared about him, as if he again sensed the presence of the cat. But then he raised his head and murmured:

'Arioch! Arioch! Why do you not come? Why do you send no messenger to us?'

For a few moments Ymryl waited expectantly, then he shook his head and continued his pacing.

Some time later Garko returned.

'The sorcerer is here, master.'

'Let him enter.'

Then there came into the room a bent figure in a long green robe decorated with writhing black serpents. Upon his face was a mask moulded to resemble the head of a striking snake. The mask was made of engraved platinum and its details were picked out in precious stones.

'Why did you summon me, Yellow Horn?' The sorcerer's voice was faintly muffled, slightly querulous, yet deferential withall. 'I was in the middle of an experiment.'

'The experiment, if it is as successful as the rest, can wait a little, Baron Kalan.'

'I suppose you are right.' The serpent mask turned this way and that as its owner glanced about the brightly lit room. 'What did you wish to discuss with me, Ymryl?'

'I wanted your opinion of our situation. My own opinion you know—that we are here because of some scheme brewed by the Lord of Chaos . . .'

'Yes. And as you know, I have no experiences of

these supernatural beings. I am a scientist. If such beings exist, then they seem devious to the point of stupidity—'

'Silence!' Ymryl raised his hand. 'I tolerate your blasphemies, Baron Kalan, because I respect your talents. I have assured you that Duke Arioch of Chaos and the rest not only exist but take a great interest in the affairs of mankind, in every sphere of existence.'

'Very well, if I must accept that notion, then I am as much at a loss as yourself to understand why they do not manifest themselves. My own theory is linked to my own experience. In my experiments in the realm of time-manipulation I caused an immense disruption which resulted, among other things, in this particular phenomenon. Like you, I sense that I am stranded here. Certainly all the efforts I have made to send my pyramid through the dimensions have met with total failure. That in itself is a problem I find hard to answer. Some conjunction of the planes has doubtless taken place—but why so many folk from so many different planes should all find themselves suddenly in this world, as we found ourselves, I do not know.'

Ymryl yawned and fingered his yellow horn. 'And that is the sum of what you have said. You do not know.'

'I assure you, Ymryl, that I am working on the problem. But I must do so in my own way—'

'Oh, I'm not blaming you, sorcerer. It seems the most ironic thing of all that there are so many clever people here and none can solve the problem. The languages we speak sound the same, but they are all essentially different. Our terms are not the same. Our references are not the same. What I call sorcery, you call "science". I speak of gods and you speak of the principles of science. They are all the same thing. Yet the words themselves confuse us.'

'You are an intelligent man, Ymryl,' Kalan said. 'I'll grant you that. I wonder why you waste your time as you do. You seem to get little relish even from your butchery, your wenching, your drinking . . .'

'You begin to go too far, even for my tolerance,' Ymryl said softly. 'I must spend my time somehow. And I've little respect for scholarship, save where it's useful. Your knowledge has proved useful to me once. I live in the patient hope that it will prove useful a second time. I am damned, you see, Baron Kalan. I know that. I was damned the instant I accepted the gift of this horn I wear about my throat. The horn that helped me rise from being the leader of a brand of cattle-thieves to be ruler of Hythiak, the most powerful nation in my world.' Ymryl smiled bleakly. 'The horn was given me by Duke Arioch himself. It summoned aid from Hell whenever I needed it. It made me great. Yet it made me, also, a slave. Slave to the Lords of Chaos. I can never relinquish their gift, just as I can never now refuse to serve them. And being damned, I see no point to life. I had ambition when I was a cattle-raider. Now I have only nostalgia for those simple days, when I spent my time drinking, killing and wenching.' And Ymryl's bleak smile widened and he laughed. 'I appear to have gained very little from my bargain.'

He put an arm around the stooped shoulders of the sorcerer and led him from the room.

'Come. I'll see how you progress with your experiments!'

The little cat crept further out onto the ledge and looked down. The two young girls still slept in each other's arms.

The cat heard Ymryl's laughter echoing back to the room. It launched itself from the ledge and flew over the bed and out through the window, heading back to where it had left Jhary-a-Conel.

CHAPTER THREE

A MEETING IN THE FOREST

'So we can anticipate a falling out, soon, amongst the invaders,' said Jhary-a-Conel. By some mysterious means the cat had communicated to him all it had seen. He stroked its small round head and it purred.

It was dawn. From the cave Katinka van Bak led three horses. Two of the horses were good, strong stallions. The third horse was Jhary's yellow nag. By now Ilian had become used to the sense of familiarity she had when she saw things she was sure she could never have seen before. She mounted one of the stallions and settled herself in the saddle, inspecting the weapons she found in the saddle sheaths—the sword and the lance with the odd, ruby tip where its point should be.

Without thinking, she looked for a grip half-way down the shaft. The grip had a jewel set into it. She knew that if she pressed the jewel destroying flame would leap from the ruby tip of the lance. Philosophically, she shrugged, glad enough to have a weapon that was as powerful as those possessed by many of Ymryl's warriors. She noticed that Katinka van Bak had a similar weapon, though Jhary's arms were of the more conventional kind, an ordinary lance, a shield and a sword.

'What of these gods in whom Ymryl pins so much faith,' Katinka asked Jhary as they rode into the massive forest, 'do they have any reality at all, Jhary?'

'They had once—or will have. I suspect that they exist when men need them to exist. But I could be wrong. Rest assured, however, Katinka van Bak, that when they do exist they are extremely powerful.'

Katinka van Bak nodded. 'Then why do they not help Ymryl?'

'It is possible that they do,' Jhary said, 'without him realising it.' He took a deep breath of the sweet air. He looked admiringly at the huge blooms, the variety of greens and browns of the trees. 'Though often these gods are unable to enter human worlds themselves and must work through agents like Ymryl. Only a powerful sorcery could bring Arioch through, I suspect.'

'And this Dark Empire lord—Baron Kalan, without a doubt—he has not sufficient skill?'

'I am sure his skill is sufficient, in his own sphere. But if he does not believe in Arioch—save, perhaps, intellectually—then he is useless to Ymryl. It is lucky for us.'

'The thought of more powerful beings than Ymryl and his pack invading Garathorm is not a pleasant one,' said Ilian. Though undisturbed by the strange half-memories which flitted through her head from time to time, she had become gloomier since she had remembered her screaming betrayal of her brother, Bradne. She had never seen his body, though she had heard there was little left of it when Ymryl's raiders brought it back to the city, for Katinka van Bak had appeared to rescue her before Ymryl could enjoy the sight of Ilian's horror.

Ymryl had guessed what would follow. She would have been so full of self-disgust that she would have agreed to any demands he made on her. She knew that she would have given herself up to him then, almost gratefully, as a means of atoning for her guilt. She drew a hissing breath as she recalled her feelings. Well, at least she had denied Ymryl the fulfilment of his scheme.

Small comfort, thought Ilian cynically. But she would have felt no better now if she had lain with Ymryl. It would not have absolved her, it would only have indulged her own sense of hysteria at the time. She could never satisfy her own conscience, for all her friends did not blame her for what she had done, but at least she could use the hatred she felt to good effect. She was determined to destroy Ymryl and all his fellows, even though she was sure such an action would result in her own destruction. That was what she wanted. She would not die before Ymryl was slain.

'We must accept the possibility that your countrymen will not reveal themselves to us,' Katinka van Bak said. 'Those who still fight Ymryl will have become wary, suspecting treachery from anyone.'

'And particularly from me,' said Ilian bitterly.

'They might not know of your brother's capture,' said Jhary. 'Or at least they might not know of the circumstances which led to his capture . . .' But the suggestion sounded weak in his own ears.

'Ymryl will have made sure all your folk will know what you did,' Katinka van Bak said. 'It would be what I would do in his position. And you can be certain that he would have had the worst interpretation put upon the facts. With the last of their hereditary rulers proven a traitress, their morale will decline and they will cause Ymryl far less trouble. I have taken cities in my time. And so, doubtless, has Ymryl taken others before Virinthorm. If he could not use you one way, Ilian, he would have used you another!'

'Any interpretation put upon my treachery could be no worse than the truth, Katinka van Bak,' said Ilian of Virinthorm.

The older woman said nothing to this. She merely pursed her lips and clapped her heels to the flanks of her horse, riding on ahead.

For the best part of the day they pressed through the tangled forest. And the deeper they went, the darker it became—a cool, green, restful darkness, full of heady scents. They were to the north east of Virinthorm and riding away from the city rather than towards it. Katinka van Bak had a feeling she knew where she might find some of the surviving Garathormians.

And at last they entered a warm, sunlit glade, blinking painfully in the bright light, and Katinka van Bak pointed to the other side of the glade.

Ilian saw dark shapes beneath the trees. Jagged shapes. And she remembered.

'Of course,' she said. 'Tikaxil! Ymryl knows nothing of the old city.'

Tikaxil had existed long before Virinthorm. It had once been a thriving trading city, home of Ilian's ancestors. A walled city. The walls had been made of huge blocks of hardwood, each block placed upon the other. Most of those blocks had disappeared now, or rotted into nothing, but a few fragments of the ramparts remained. And there were one or two ebony houses which, for all they were thickly wound about with creepers and low branches, were almost as good as when they had been built.

In the middle of the glade the three stopped and dismounted, looking warily around them. Overhead massive tree branches waved and mottled shadows skipped across the grass.

Ilian kept seeing the moving shadows as figures. It was possible that Ymryl's men and not her own folk were camped here—if anyone was camped here at all.

She kept her hand near the oddly familiar flame-lance, ready to meet an attack.

Katinka van Bak spoke clearly.

'If you are friends of ours you will recognise us. You will know that we come to ally ourselves with you against Ymryl.'

'The place is deserted,' said Jhary-a-Conel, dismounted from his yellow nag and looking about him. 'But it will make a good place to camp tonight.'

'See—this is your queen, Ilian, Pyran's daughter. Remember how she bore the burning banner into battle with Ymryl's army? And I am Katinka van Bak, also known to you as Ymryl's enemy. This is Jhary-a-Conel. Without his help, your queen would not be here now.'

'You speak to birds and squirrels, Katinka van Bak,' said Jhary-a-Conel. 'There are none here from Garathorm.'

He had not finished this sentence before the nets swept and engulfed them. It was a tribute to the training of each of them that they did not struggle but calmly attempted to draw their swords, to cut their way free. But Katinka and Ilian were still mounted. Ilian tried to slash her way clear, but her horse kept rearing and whinnying in fear. Only Jhary was unmounted and he managed to crawl under the edge of the net and be ready with his sword as a score of men and women, all armed, came rushing at them from behind the ruined ramparts.

Ilian's arms became increasingly entangled in the tough fibres of the net and, as she struggled, she found herself slipping from the saddle and falling to the ground.

She felt someone kick her in the stomach. She gasped

in pain, hearing someone snarling insults at her, though she could not make out the words.

Katinka van Bak had misjudged the situation, obviously. These folk were not friends.

CHAPTER FOUR

A PACT IS MADE

'You are fools!' said Katinka van Bak contemptuously. 'You do not deserve the chance we offer. Ymryl's plans are well suited by your actions. Do you not realise that you are doing exactly what he would want you to do?'

'Silence!' The young man with the scar along his jaw glared at her.

Ilian raised her head, feebly shaking it to free the strands of hair which clung to the sweat on her face. 'Why reason with them, Katinka? They are right from their point of view.'

They had been hanging by their arms for the best part of three days, being released only to eat and relieve themselves. For all the pain involved, it was nothing compared with what Ilian had suffered in Ymryl's dungeons. She was hardly aware of the discomfort. And their captors had concentrated most of their spleen on her. She had received several kicks since the first. She had been spat upon, slapped, reviled. It meant nothing to her. It was her due, that was all.

'They'll destroy themselves if they destroy us,' said Jhary-a-Conel quietly. He, too, seemed hardly to notice the pain. He seemed to have been sleeping through most of their ordeal. His black and white cat had vanished.

The young man looked from Ilian to Katinka to

Jhary. 'We are doomed anyway,' he said. 'It will not be long before Ymryl's hounds sniff us out.'

'That is my point,' said Katinka van Bak.

Ilian looked across the ruins of the old city. Attracted by the sound of voices the others were coming over to the tree where the three prisoners hung. Ilian recognised many of the faces. These were the young people with whom she had spent so much time in the old days. These were the trained fighters, those who had resisted Ymryl longest, as well as a few citizens who had either managed to escape from Virinthorm or who had not been near the city when Ymryl had captured it. And there was not one there who did not hate her with that hatred that only comes from those who have admired someone and then discovered that person to be despicable.

'There is not one here who would not have given the information Ilian gave Ymryl,' said Katinka. 'You must know little of life if you do not understand that. You are still soft, you fighters. You are not realistic. We are the only chance you have of fighting Ymryl and winning. To misuse us so is to misuse your assets. Forget your hatred of Ilian—at least until we have fought Ymryl. You have insufficient resources, my friends, to discard the best!'

The young man with the scar was called Mysenal of Hinn and he was a distant relative of Ilian's. Once, Ilian knew, he had had an infatuation for her, as had many other young men of the court. Mysenal frowned. 'Your words are sensible, Katinka van Bak, and you have advised us well in the past. But how do we know that these sensible words are not being used to deceive us. For all we know you've made some bargain with Ymryl to deliver us into his hands.'

'You must remember that I am Katinka van Bak. I would not do such a thing.'

'Queen Ilian betrayed her own brother,' Mysenal reminded Katinka.

Ilian closed her eyes. Now there was pain, but not from the ropes which chafed her wrists.

'Under abominable torture,' Katinka pointed out impatiently. 'Just as, perhaps, I would have done. Have you any notion of Ymryl's skills in that quarter?'

'Some,' Mysenal admitted. 'Yet . . .'

'And why, if we were in league with Ymryl, would we come here alone? If we knew where you camped, we had merely to tell him. He could have sent a force to destroy you and caught you by surprise . . .'

'Not by surprise. There are guards in the high branches for more than a mile in all directions. We should have known and we should have fled. We knew you were coming and had time to prepare for you, had we not?'

'True. But my point is still valid.'

Mysenal of Hinn sighed. 'Some of us would rather have vengeance on this traitress than fight Ymryl. Some of us feel we should try to make a life for ourselves here, in the hope that Ymryl will forget us.'

'He will not. He is bored. It will please him, soon, to hunt you down himself. You are only tolerated at present because he thought that those who conquered the west were readying themselves to attack Virinthorm. Thus he kept most of his forces in the city. But now he knows that the west does not immediately prepare to march. He will be reminded of you.'

'The invaders quarrel amongst themselves?' Mysenal's voice became interested. 'They fight each other?'

'Not yet. But it is inevitable. I see you realise the

implications of that. It is what we came to tell you, among other things.'

'If they fall upon each other, then we have a better chance of striking effectively at those who took Virinthorm!' Mysenal rubbed at his scar. 'Aye.' Then he frowned again. 'But this information could be part of your ruse to deceive us . . .'

'It is a complicated interpretation, I'll give you that,' said Jhary-a-Conel wearily. 'Why not accept that we came to join with you against Ymryl. It is the most likely explanation.'

'I believe them.' It was a girl who spoke. Ilian's old friend Lyfeth, who had been her brother's lover.

Lyfeth's words carried weight with the others. After all, Lyfeth had most to hate Ilian for.

'I think we should cut them down, for a while at least. We should listen to everything they have to say. Katinka van Bak is responsible for us being able to put up at least a little resistance to Ymryl, remember that. And we have no grudge against the other fellow, Jhary-a-Conel, at all. Also it could be that—that Ilian—' Lyfeth plainly found it hard even to speak Ilian's name—'would make amends for her treachery. I cannot say that I would not have betrayed Bradne if subjected to the tortures Katinka van Bak has described. I knew her once as a friend. I thought highly of her, as did we all. She fought well in her father's stead. Yes, I think I am prepared to trust her, with a certain amount of caution.'

Lyfeth advanced to where Ilian hung.

Ilian dropped her head and closed her eyes again, unable to look into Lyfeth's face.

But Lyfeth stretched out a hard hand and grasped Ilian under the chin, harshly forcing her head up.

Ilian opened her eyes and tried to stare back at Lyfeth. Lyfeth's own eyes were enigmatic. There was hatred there, but also sympathy.

'Hate me, Lyfeth of Ghant,' said Ilian, for Lyfeth's ears only. 'You need do no more. But listen to me, also, for I do not come to betray you.'

Lyfeth bit her lower lip. Once she had been beautiful —more beautiful than Ilian—but now her face had hardened and her skin was pale, rough. Her hair had been cut short, to the nape of her neck. She wore no ornament. Her patched smock was green, to blend with the foliage, and belted at the waist with a broad, woven belt, at which hung her sword and dagger. Her legs were bare and she wore tough-soled sandals on her feet. Her garb was no different from that worn by most here. With her chain-mail jerkin and leggings, Ilian felt almost overdressed.

'Whether you came to betray us or not this time, that's not important,' said Lyfeth. 'For there would still be every reason to punish you for Bradne's death. An uncivilised opinion, I know, Ilian. But I feel it strongly. However, if you have the means of defeating Ymryl, then we should listen to you. Katinka van Bak's reasoning is good.' Lyfeth turned away, letting Ilian's head drop again. 'Cut them down!'

'The Yellow Horn will soon make plans to attack the west,' said Jhary-a-Conel. His cat had returned to his shoulder and he stroked it absently as he told Mysenal and the others of all he had discovered through its help. 'Who rules in the west now, do you know?'

'One called Kagat Bearclaw had the cities of Bekthorm and Rivensz under his sway,' said Lyfeth, 'but more recent news suggests that he was murdered by a rival and that two or three rule there now, among them one called Arnald of Grovent, who has little resemblance

to a man, but is blessed with the body of a lion and
the face of an ape, though he walks on two legs.'

'A Chaos creature,' mused Jhary-a-Conel. 'There are
so many here. It is as if Garathorm has become a world
to which all those who serve Chaos are banished! An
unpleasant thought.'

There had been two other large cities in the west,
Ilian recalled. 'What of Poytarn and Masgha?' she asked.

Mysenal looked surprised. 'You have not heard. A
vast explosion destroyed Masgha—and destroyed all
those within it. It was nought to do with those who resist the conquerors, by all accounts. They destroyed
themselves, by accident. Some sorcerous experiment, no
doubt.'

'And Poytarn?'

'Looted, razed and abandoned. Those who did it
rode to the coast, doubtless hoping to find other rich
pickings. They'll be disappointed. The sea villages would
be deserted. Those who lived on the coast were the
luckiest of us. Many were able to put to sea and escape to distant islands before the invaders found them.
The invaders have no ships and thus could not pursue
them. I hope they fare well. We would attempt to follow them, if there were any ships left.'

'They have made counter-attacks?'

'Not yet,' said Lyfeth. 'Soon, we hope.'

'Or not at all,' said someone else. 'They probably have
enough sense to bide their time—or merely forget the
problems of the mainland.'

'Still, they are potential allies,' said Katinka van Bak.
'I had not realised so many had escaped.'

'But we cannot contact them,' Lyfeth pointed out
patiently. 'No ships.'

'There might be other means devised. But we must
consider that later.'

Ilian said: 'It seems to me that Ymryl places much faith in that yellow horn he wears ever about his neck. If that could be stolen from him or destroyed by some means, it would weaken his confidence. Perhaps he even draws his power from the horn, as he believes. If so, there would be even more reason to part him from it.'

'A good thought,' said Mysenal. 'But hard to accomplish. Would you not say so, Katinka van Bak?'

Katinka nodded. 'However, it is an important factor, and something we must continue to consider.' She sniffed and rubbed at her nose. 'The first thing we need are some better weapons than these. Something a little more modern, in my terms. Flame-lances and the like. If each of us was armed with a flame-lance, we should immediately triple our striking power. How many are here, Lyfeth?'

'Fifth-three.'

'So we need fifty-four good weapons—the extra one being for Jhary here, who has weapons as primitive as yours. Weapons which depend upon a power source . . .'

'I follow your reasoning,' Jhary said. 'You see a certain expenditure of resources by Ymryl and the others, when they eventually do war on each other. If we are then in possession of weapons like flame-lances, we shall have a considerable advantage, no matter how small our numbers.'

'Exactly. But the problem is how to capture such a large supply, eh?'

'It could mean a visit to Garathorm itself,' said Ilian. She stood up, stretching her bruised muscles and wincing. She had stripped off her chain armour and was now dressed in a green smock like the others. She had made every effort to show her ex-friends that she wished to be accepted as one of them. 'For that is where we should find such weapons.'

'And death,' said Lyfeth. 'We should find death there, too.'

'We should have to disguise ourselves.' Katinka van Bak stroked her lips.

'Better,' said Jhary-a-Conel, 'we should bring the weapons to us.'

'What do you mean?' Ilian asked him.

CHAPTER FIVE

THE RAID ON VIRINTHORM

There were eight.

Ilian was in the fore. She was dressed again in her shining chain armour, with her helmet on her golden hair, a slender sword in her gauntleted hand.

She led the remaining seven along the wide branches of the trees, balancing expertly, for she had trodden the tree-roads since she was a child.

Virinthorm was ahead.

Slung on her back was one of their two flame-lances. The other was back at the camp, with Katinka van Bak.

Ilian paused as they reached the outskirts of Virinthorm and could see the city's conquerors moving about in the streets.

Virinhorm had, over the months, become a series of smaller townships. Each township attracted groups or races of men or other creatures to it, so that those from similar eras or similar worlds or those who resembled each other physically would band together.

The township on which Ilian and her small band now spied was one which they had selected specially. It was made up mainly of folk who resembled mankind in many ways and yet who were not men.

The features of these people—who were drawn from many spheres and eras—were familiar to Ilian. Indeed, now that she looked upon them, she had a great re-

luctance to put her plan into action. They were tall and
slender, with slanting, almond eyes, ears which came
almost to points. While the eyes of some of them were
like those of ordinary men, others had eyes that were
purple and yellow, others had eyes that were flecks of
blue and silver which sparkled constantly. They seemed
a proud and intelligent people and were plainly given to
avoiding most of their fellows. Yet Ilian also knew that
these could be cruellest of all the invaders.

'Call them Eldren, call them Vadhagh, call them
Melniboneans,' Jhary-a-Conel had said to her, 'but remember that these are renegades all of some kind, else
they would not league themselves with Ymryl. And
doubtless they also serve Chaos as willingly as docs
Ymryl. Feel no regret for what you do.'

Ilian drew the flame-lance off her back, then began to
work her way round to the far side of the unhumans'
enclave. On this side dwelled a group of warriors who
had all been born at the end of or immediately after the
Tragic Millenium. As a group, they were one of the
best armed. Each man had at least one flame-lance.

It was about an hour to dusk. Ilian judged her moment the right one. She picked out an unhuman warrior
at random, pointed the flame-lance with a skill she had
no right to possess and touched the jewelled stud. Immediately a beam of red light issued from the ruby tip
and burned a clean hole through the breastplate of the
warrior, through his torso and through the backplate on
the other side. Ilian released the stud and moved back
into the leafier branches to watch what would happen
next.

Already a crowd had gathered around the corpse.
Many of the eldritch-featured men pointed at once
towards the neighbouring camp. Swords slipped from
scabbards. Ilian heard oaths, a babble of rage. Her plan

had worked so far. The unhumans had drawn the obvious conclusion that one of their number had been murdered by those to whom the flame-lance was their first weapon.

Leaving the corpse where it lay about thirty of the unhumans, all dressed in a variety of styles of clothing and armour, each looking faintly different to the other, began to run towards the neighbouring camp.

Ilian smiled as she watched them. Her old pleasure in fighting and tactics was returning.

She saw the unhumans gesticulating as they reached the other camp. She saw warriors come running out of their houses, buckling on swords. She knew that Ymryl had banned the use of power weapons within the confines of the camp and that this made the crime doubly treacherous. Yet she did not expect a fully-fledged fight to develop yet. She had noticed that the discipline of the camp though crude was effective and designed to stop such squabbles between different factions.

Now Tragic Millenium swords flashed in the dying light of the sun, but still they were not used. A man who was obviously the leader of the unhumans was deep in argument with the chief of the humans. Then both groups trooped back to the unhumans' camp to inspect the corpse. Again the Tragic Millenium leader was plainly denying that his men had anything to do with the murder. He indicated that they were all only armed with swords and knives. Still the unhuman leader was not mollified. The source of the beam seemed obvious to him. Then the human chief pointed in the direction of his own camp and again the warriors stalked across the space between their camps. Here the human pointed to a sturdily built house whose doors and windows were heavily padlocked. He sent one of his men away. The man returned with a bunch of keys. The keys were

used to open one of the doors. By straining her eyes
Ilian could just see inside. As she had hoped, this was
the house where the flame-lances were stored. It was
one of the necessary things she had to know before she
could continue. Now, as the two factions separated, not
without exchanging many scowls, she and her band settled down to wait for night.

They lay in the boughs overlooking the Tragic
Millenium camp, almost directly over the flame-lance
storehouse.

Ilian signed to the nearest youth who nodded and
drew an exquisitely made dagger from his shirt. This
was a captured dagger, belonging to the unhumans.
Silently, the young man dropped down through the trees
until he stood in the shadows of the street. He waited for
nearly half-an-hour before a warrior came strolling by.
Then he leapt from the dark. One arm went around the
throat of the warrior. The dagger rose. The dagger fell.
The warrior screamed. Again the dagger struck. Again
the warrior screamed. The young man was not striking
for the death, but to inflict pain, to force the warrior to
yell out.

The third blow was the death blow. The dagger jutted
through the man's throat as his corpse fell to the ground.
The youth jumped up and began to climb up the side
of a house, jumping into the lower branches of a tree
and then disappearing as he climbed higher to rejoin his
comrades.

This time the scene was enacted from the point of
view of the Tragic Millenium soldiers who came running
to discover the body with the unhuman dagger sticking
in its throat.

It was obvious to them what happened. In spite of
their innocence. In spite of their protestations, the un-

humans had taken a cowardly vengeance on them for a crime they could not possibly have committed.

As one man the Tragic Millenium soldiers raced towards the unhumans' camp.

And that was when Ilian dropped from her tree onto the roof of the armoury. Swiftly she slung her own flame-lance from her back and directed its beam close to her feet, cutting a circle large enough to admit her body. Meanwhile the others had joined her on the roof. One of them held her flame-lance as she lowered herself into the building.

She was in a loft. The lances were plainly stored in the rooms below. She found a trap-door and eased it open, dropping into deeper darkness. Slowly her eyes became used to the gloom. A little light came through chinks in the shutters on the windows. She had found some of the lances, at least. She went back the way she had come and signalled for all but one of her band to follow her. While they began to remove the lances, forming a human chain to take them out of the opening she had carved, she explored the lower rooms, finding more lances there, as well as a variety of edged weapons, including some fine throwing axes. These she had to ignore, and it would not be possible to steal more than sixty or so of the lances in the time they had, for there was also the question of carrying them back to their own camp. As she turned to go something came to mind. How did she know that the tips of the lances unscrewed from their shafts? She did not stop to wonder on this but crossed to where she had seen the lances stacked and began to unscrew the ruby tips. As she unscrewed them she picked up a well-balanced axe, placed the tip upon the floor and smashed the axe not on the ruby, which would not break, but upon the stem which screwed into the shaft, denting

it so that they would have considerable difficulty in re-
pairing their lances. It was the best she could do.

She heard voices outside. She crossed silently to the
nearest window and looked down.

Other soldiers had appeared in the street. These
looked like those Ymryl had made into his personal
guard. They had doubtless been sent to quell the trouble.
Ilian admired Ymryl's efficiency. He never seemed to
care about such things, yet he always reacted swiftly
when there was any danger of disruption in his camp.
Already the soldiers were yelling at the embattled unhumans and Tragic Millenium humans, forcing them to
lay down their weapons.

Ilian climbed back to where her band was getting the
last of the flame-lances through the hole.

'Go,' she whispered. 'The danger increases. Leave
now.'

'You, Queen Ilian?' said the youth who had killed
the soldier.

'I'll follow. There is something I must try to finish
here.'

She watched until the last of her band had disappeared and then she went back to unscrew the tips of
the few remaining flame-lances. Smashing the axe down
on the last, she heard a yell, a commotion. Again she
peered through the crack in the shutter.

Men were pointing at the roof of the building. Ilian
looked round for her own flame-lance and then realised
that it had gone with her comrades. She had only her
sword. She ran up the stairs, reached the loft, jumped
and swung up through the hole she had herself made.

They had seen her.

And that was when an arrow whistled past her shoulder, so close that involuntarily she ducked back, lost her
footing on the roof beam and fell down the sloping

roof towards the ground on the other side of the house.
But men were already running here. She managed to
grasp a gable as she went over the edge. Her arms were
almost pulled from her body as she swung there with
arrows whistling on all sides. One or two arrows struck
her helmet and mail, but did not penetrate. She got a
foothold somewhere and pushed herself back up again,
crouching behind the gable as she ran along, searching
for a branch low enough to jump for. But there was no
such branch. Now figures were appearing above her.
They had found what had happened to their weapons
and where she had entered. She could hear their angry
shouts and she was glad she had gone back to destroy
every one of the flame-lances. If they had had them now,
she would be dead already. She reached the far end
of the roof and prepared to jump to the next. It was
her only means of escape.

She launched herself into space, hands clutching for
the gable of that house. She grasped the carved wood
and felt it give sickeningly beneath her weight. She hung
there, thinking she would fall, but the gable held and
she hauled herself up. They had realised where she was
and more arrows sought her. She jumped from that roof
to another, closer, realising with despair that she was
moving deeper and deeper into the city as they pursued
her. She prayed that she would eventually come to a
spot where a branch brushed the roofs. In the trees she
had a much better chance of escape. She was con-
soled, at least, that her comrades were getting away in
the other direction.

Three more roofs and they had lost her for the moment. She breathed in relief. But it was a matter of time
before they caught her, she was sure.

If she could get into one of the houses and hide,
then they would assume she had escaped. When the pur-

suit died down it would not be too difficult to leave at her leisure.

She saw an unlit house ahead.

That would do.

She jumped across the gap between the roofs, landed, swung over the edge of the roof and down to a window ledge. Crouching on the ledge she forced open the shutters and crept in, drawing the shutters to behind her.

She was tired. The chain-mail was heavy on her body. She wished she had time to remove it. Without it she could jump higher, climb faster. But it was too late to worry about such things now.

The room in which she found herself smelled musky as if the windows had not been opened for a long time. As she moved across it, she bumped her knee against something. A chest? A bed?

And then she heard a stifled moan.

Ilian peered into the gloom.

A figure lay upon a rumpled bed. It was the figure of a woman.

And she was bound.

Was this some fellow-citizen whom one of the invaders was keeping prisoner? Ilian bent forward to remove the gag which had been tightly drawn about the girl's mouth.

'Who are you?' Ilian whispered. 'Do not fear me. I'll save you if that's possible, though I'm in great danger myself.'

And then Ilian gasped as the gag came free.

She recognised the face.

It was the face of a ghost.

Ilian felt terror shiver through her body. It was a terror that she could not name. A terror which she had never felt before, for while she recognized the face, she could not name it.

Neither could she remember where, in all her life, she had seen it before.

She tried to stop her impulse to shrink away from the bound figure on the bed.

'Who are you?' said the woman.

CHAPTER SIX

THE WRONG CHAMPION

Ilian controlled herself. She found a lamp, found flint and tinder and lit the lamp while she took deep breaths and tried to rationalise what was happening to her. The shock of recognition had been strong—yet she could swear she had never seen the woman before.

Ilian turned. The woman was dressed in a filthy white gown. She had evidently been kept prisoner here for some time. She began to try to struggle into a sitting position on the bed. Her hands were locked in front of her, in a complicated leather harness which also bound her throat, her legs and her feet.

Ilian wondered if this were a madwoman. Perhaps it had been foolish to cut the gag without thinking. There was something wild about the woman's eyes, but again that could merely be because she had been captive so long.

'Are you of Garathorm?' Ilian asked, holding up the lamp to peer once more at the woman's pale features.

'Garathorm? This place? No.'

'You seem familiar.'

'You, also. Yet . . .'

'Aye,' said Ilian feelingly. 'You have never seen me before either.'

'My name is Yisselda of Brass. I am Baron Kalan's captive and have been since I came here.'

'Why are you his prisoner?'

'He is afraid I might escape and be seen. He wants me for himself. I seem to represent some sort of talisman for him. He has done me no great harm. Can you cut this harness, do you think?'

Reassured by Yisselda of Brass's level tones, Ilian bent and sliced through the straps. Yisselda gasped as feeling returned to her limbs. 'I thank you.'

'I am Ilian of Garathorm. Queen Ilian.'

'King Pyran's daughter!' Yisselda seemed astonished. 'But Kalan drew your soul from you, did he not?'

'So I gather. But I have a new soul now.'

'Indeed?'

Ilian smiled. 'Do not ask me to explain. So not all who came so suddenly to our world are evil.'

'Most are those whom we should call evil. Most are pledged to Chaos, Kalan tells me, and believe they cannot be slain. But he hardly believes that theory himself. It is what he is told.'

Ilian was trembling, wondering why she had the impulse to embrace this woman, to hold her in a way that was more than comradely. She had never felt such impulses before. Her knees shook. Without thinking, she sat down on the bed.

'Fate,' she murmured. 'They say I serve Fate. Do you know aught of that, Yisselda of Brass? I know your name so well—and that of Baron Kalan. It seems to me I have been searching for you—searching all my life—and yet it is not I who searched. Oh . . .' She was close to fainting. She put a hand to her brow. 'This is horrifying.'

'I understand you. Kalan thinks that his experiments in time distortion have created this situation. Our lives are mixed up so much. One possibility clashes with another. It must even be possible to meet oneself, under these conditions.'

'Kalan was responsible for letting Ymryl and the rest through?'

'So he believes. He spends his whole time trying to restore the balance which he himself disrupted. And I am important to him in his experiments. He has no wish to go with Ymryl on the morrow.'

'Tomorrow? Where does Ymryl ride?'

'Against the west. Against one called Arnald of Grovent, I understand.'

'So they fight at last!' Ilian forgot everything but that fact for a moment. She was exhilarated. Their opportunity was coming sooner than she had hoped.

'Baron Kalan is Ymryl's mascot,' said Yisselda. She had found a comb somewhere and was trying to comb out her tangled hair. 'Just as I am Kalan's. I survive thanks to a chain of superstition!'

'And where is Kalan now?'

'Doubtless in Ymryl's palace—your father's palace, is it not?'

'It is. What does he there?'

'Some of his experiments. Ymryl has set him up with a laboratory, though really Kalan prefers to work from here. He will take me with him when he works, sitting me down and talking to me as if I were a pet dog. It is the most attention he pays me. Needless to say I understand little of what he talks about. I was present, however, when he stole your soul. That was horrible. How did you recover it?'

Ilian did not answer. 'How did he—steal my soul?'

'With a jewel, similar to that which threatened to eat my Hawkmoon's brain when it was imbedded in his skull. A jewel of similar properties, at any rate . . .'

'Hawkmoon? That name . . .'

'Aye? You know Hawkmoon. How does he fare? Surely he is not in this world . . .?'

'No—no. I do not know him. I do not know why I should. Yet it sounded so familiar.'

'You are unwell, Ilian of Garathorm?'

'Aye. Aye. I could be.' Ilian felt faint. Doubtless the exertions she had had to make to escape Ymryl's soldiers had tired her more than she had at first realised. Again she made an effort to recover. 'This jewel, then? Kalan has it? And my soul, he believes, is in it?'

'Yes. But he is plainly wrong. Somehow your soul was released from the jewel.'

'Plainly,' Ilian smiled grimly. 'Well, we must consider a means of escaping. You do not look fit enough to climb rooftops and swing through trees with me.'

'I can try,' said Yisselda. 'I am stronger than I seem.'

'Then we must try, then. When do you expect Kalan's return?'

'He only recently left.'

'Then we have some time. I will use it in resting.' Ilian leaned back on the bed. 'My head aches so.'

Yisselda reached forward to massage Ilian's brow, but Ilian drew away with a gasp. 'No!' She licked dry lips. 'No. I thank you for your consideration.'

Yisselda went to the still shuttered window and cautiously opened it a little, breathing in the cooler night air.

'Kalan is to try to help Ymryl make contact with this black god of his, this Arioch.'

'Whom Ymryl believes responsible for placing him here?'

'Yes. Ymryl will blow that Yellow Horn he has and Kalan will try to concoct some form of spell. Kalan is cynical concerning their chances of raising the demon.'

'Ymryl's horn is dear to him. Does he never let it off his person?'

'Never, so Kalan says. The only one who could make Ymryl give up his horn is Arioch himself.'

The time passed with painful slowness. While Ilian tried to rest, Yisselda extinguished the lamp and watched the streets, noticing that patrols of soldiers still searched there for Ilian. Some were even on the roof-tops at one stage. But eventually they seemed to have given up the search and Yisselda went to rouse Ilian, who was by now sleeping fitfully.

Yisselda shook Ilian's shoulder and Ilian shuddered, waking with a start.

'They are gone,' said Yisselda. 'I think we can risk leaving. How shall we go? Into the street?'

'No. But a coil of rope would help. Is there one in the house, do you think?'

'I will see.'

Yisselda returned in a few minutes with a length of rope coiled over her shoulder. 'It is the longest I could find. Is it strong enough?'

'It will have to be.' Ilian smiled. She opened the window wide and looked up. The nearest large branch was some ten feet overhead. Ilian took the rope and made a noose at one end, coiling the rope so that it was the same circumference as the noose. Then she began to swing the coil round and round before releasing it suddenly.

The noose settled over a branch, held, and Ilian tightened the knot.

'You'll have to climb onto my back,' Ilian told Yisselda, 'curling your legs around my waist and hanging on as hard as you can. Do you think you'll be able to?'

'I must,' said Yisselda simply. She did as she was ordered and then Ilian pulled herself onto the window sill, took a good grip on the rope, turning it round her hand once or twice, and then flung herself out over the rooftops, narrowly missing the spire of one of the old trading halls. Her feet struck another branch and she dug in her heels, straining with all her might to get a better grip on the branch above her. She was about to slip when Yisselda reached up and pulled herself onto the branch, leaning down to help Ilian after her. They lay panting on the great branch.

Ilian sprang up. 'Follow me,' she said. 'Keep your arms spread for balance. And keep moving.'

She began to run along the bole.

And Yisselda, somewhat shakily, followed her.

They were back at the camp by morning and they were jubilant.

Katinka van Bak came out of the shack she had built for herself from old planks and she was delighted to see Ilian. 'We feared for you,' she said. 'Even those who profess to hate you so. The others came back with the flame-lances. A good haul.'

'Excellent. And I have more information.'

'Good. Good. You'll want to breakfast—and rest, too, I should think. Who is this?' Katinka van Bak seemed to notice the woman in the white, soiled dress for the first time.

'She is called Yisselda of Brass. She, like you, is not of Garathorm . . .'

Ilian noticed the look of astonishment which appeared on Katinka's face then. 'Yisselda? Count Brass's daughter?'

'Aye,' said Yisselda in some delight. 'Though Count Brass is dead—slain at the Battle of Londra.'

'Not so! Not so! He dwells still at Castle Brass! So Hawkmoon was right. You are alive! This is the strangest thing I have yet to experience—but by far the most pleasurable.'

'You have seen Dorian? How is he?'

'Ah—' Katinka van Bak seemed to become evasive. 'He is well. He is well. He has been ill, but now all the portents are that he will recover.'

'I wish it was possible to see him again. He is not in this plane?'

'Unfortunately he could not be.'

'How came you here? In the same manner as myself?'

'Pretty much the same, aye.' Katinka van Bak turned to see that Jhary-a-Conel had emerged from one of the ebony houses still standing. He was rubbing sleep from his eyes and looked barely awake. 'Jhary. This is Yisselda of Brass. Hawkmoon was right.'

'She is alive!' Jhary slapped his thigh, looking with some irony from Ilian to Yisselda and back again. 'Ha! This is the best I've ever known! Oh, dear!' And he burst into laughter which Ilian and Yisselda found inexplicable.

Ilian felt anger rise in her. 'I become bored with your mysteries and your hints, Sir Jhary! I become bored with them!'

'Aye!' Jhary continued to laugh. 'I think it is the best way to respond to it all, madam!'

BOOK THREE

A LEAVETAKING

CHAPTER ONE

SWEET BATTLE, TRIUMPHANT VENGEANCE

There were nearly a hundred of them now and most of them had flame-lances. They had been hastily trained in the use of the lances by Katinka van Bak and some of the lances were inclined to be faulty, for they were very old, but the weapons gave confidence to all who bore them.

Ilian turned in her saddle to look back at her troops. Each man and woman was mounted, mostly on striding *vayna* birds. Each hailed the burning banner as she turned. The fiery thing, which burned without consuming the cloth, fluttered over her armoured head. It was their pride. And they were going to Virinthorm.

Beneath the great, green trees of Garathorm they rode: Ilian, Katinka van Bak, Jhary-a-Conel, Yisselda of Brass, Lyfeth of Ghant, Mysenal of Hinn and the rest. All, save Katinka van Bak, were youthful.

It seemed to Ilian that, while her own crimes had not been forgotten by those she led, she and her people were united again. But much would depend on how they fared in the battles which lay ahead.

They rode through the morning and by the afternoon they had come in sight of Virinthorm.

Spies had already reported the departure of Ymryl with his main force. He had left less than a quarter of his men behind to defend Virinthorm, not expecting any

kind of full scale attack. Yet still those defenders were
some five hundred strong and would have been more
than sufficient to defeat Ilian's force, had they not been
armed with flame-lances.

Yet even the flame-lances only improved the chances
of the Garathormians. It was by no means certain that
they would defeat Ymryl's men. This, however, was the
only chance they might have to try.

And they sang as they rode. They sang the old songs
of their land. Gay songs, full of their love for their rich,
arboreal world. They hardly paused as they reached the
suburbs of Virinthorm and spread out.

Ymryl's men had garrisoned themselves close to the
centre of the town, near the large house which had once
been the residence of Ilian's family, and which had,
until lately, become Ymryl's palace.

Ilian regretted that Ymryl himself was not there. She
looked forward to taking her vengeance on him, should
her schemes be successful.

Now the hundred riders, thinly spread, had dismounted and situated themselves in a circle around the
centre of the city. Some lay behind roughly thrown up
barricades, others lay on roofs, while still others
crouched in doorways. A hundred flame-lances were
aimed into the city when Ilian rode out into the broad
main avenue and cried:

'Surrender in the name of Queen Ilian!'

And her voice was high and proud.

'Surrender, Ymryl's men! We have returned to claim
our city.'

The few who were on the streets turned to look in
consternation, hands reaching for weapons. Men in
every form of clothing, in all sorts of armour, in a score
of different shapes, men with fur all over their bodies,
men who were completely hairless, men with four arms

or four legs, men with beastlike heads, men with tails
or horns or tufted ears, men with hooves instead of
feet, men with green, blue, red and black skins, men
armed with bizarre weapons, the purpose of which was
mysterious, men deformed, men who were dwarves and
men who were giants, hermaphrodites, men with wings
or with transparent skins, came pouring into the streets
and saw Queen Ilian of Garathorm and laughed.

A warrior with an orange beard which came to a
point at his belt called out:

'Ilian is dead. As you will be before another minute
has passed.'

In reply Ilian raised her flame-lance, touched the
jewelled stud, and pierced the man's forehead with a
beam of red light, whereupon a dog-faced soldier
threw a disc which howled and which Ilian was barely
able to deflect by bringing up the small buckler she had
on her right arm. She wheeled her horse around and
dashed for cover. Behind her the defenders also sought
cover as beams of red light darted at them from all
around.

For an hour the fight raged thus, with either side
using power weapons from cover, while Katinka van
Bak rode from warrior to warrior, giving instructions
to tighten the circle and contain the defenders in as
small an area as possible. This they did, not without
considerable difficulty, for though the enemy had fewer
power weapons, they were more skilled in using them.

Ilian climbed a rooftop to see how the battle went. She
had lost about ten of her small band, but Ymryl's men
had lost more. She counted at least forty corpses. But
the alien soldiers were plainly grouping for a counter-
attack. Many had mounted themselves on a variety of
beasts, including some captured *vayna*.

Ilian dropped back down to the ground and sought

Katinka van Bak. 'They are planning to charge through, Katinka!'

'Then they must be stopped,' said the warrior woman, firmly.

Ilian got back onto her own *vayna*. The long-legged bird croaked as Ilian swung it round. It began to stride away to where Jhary-a-Conel had taken up his position in the window of a house looking towards the central square.

'Jhary! They charge!' she called.

And then a packed mass of cavalry came howling along the avenue and it seemed to Ilian for a moment that only she stood against it.

She raised her flame-lance, touched the stud. Ruby light flared, flickered from the hip, cut an erratic swathe across the bodies of the leading riders. In going down, they got in the way of those behind them and the force of the charge was weakened.

But the lance was now all but useless. The light wavered, spread, merely burned the skins of the soldiers as the sun might burn them, and they came on.

Ilian flung down the lance, drew her slender sword, took her long poignard in the hand that also held her reins, and urged the *vayna* forward. Behind her, in its saddle rest, the burning banner cracked and hissed as she gathered speed.

'For Garathorm!'

And now she knew joy. A black joy. A terrible joy.

'For Pyran and Bradne!'

And her sword sliced through the transparent flesh of a ghostly creature who grinned at her and tried to slash her with steel claws.

'For vengeance!'

And how sweet it was, that vengeance. How satisfying, that blood-letting. So close to death was she, and yet she felt more alive than she had ever felt. This was her destiny—to bear a sword into battle—to fight—to kill.

And as she fought it seemed she did not mercly fight this battle but a thousand others. And in each battle she had another name, yet in each battle she felt the same grim elation.

Around her the enemy roared and rattled and it seemed that a score of swords forever sought to slay her, but she laughed at them.

And her laughter was a weapon. It chilled the blood of those she fought. It filled them with a great and unwholesome terror.

'For Fate's soldier!' she heard herself shouting. 'For the Champion Eternal. For the Struggle Without End!' And she knew not the meaning of the words, though she knew she had cried them before and would cry them again, whether she survived this encounter or not.

Now others were joining her. She saw Jhary-a-Conel's yellow horse rearing and snorting and thrashing out with its hooves, striking down warriors on all sides. The horse seemed possessed of unnatural intelligence. Its actions were no mere flailing, no panicky defence. It fought aggressively, with its master. And it grinned, displaying crooked yellow teeth, cold yellow eyes, while its rider slashed this way and that with his sword, a small smile on his lips.

And there was Katinka van Bak, tough, methodical and cool as she went about the business of slaying. She held a double-bladed battle-axe in one gloved hand, a spiked mace in the other, for she did not consider the situation suitable for the subtler sword-work. She pushed her heavy, stolid horse deep into the enemy and she chopped off limbs and crushed skulls just as surely as a housewife might prepare meat and vegetables for her husband's meal. And Katinka van Bak did not smile. She took her work seriously, doing what had to be done and feeling neither disgust nor relish.

Ilian wondered at the relish she herself felt. Her whole body tingled with pleasure. She should have been weary, but instead she felt fresher than she had ever felt before.

'For Garathorm! For Pyran! For Bradne!'

'For Bradne!' echoed a voice behind her. 'And for Ilian!'

It was Lyfeth of Ghant, wielding her sword with a mixture of delicacy and ferocity which came close to matching Ilian's own. And nearby was Yisselda of Brass, proving herself an experienced warrior, using the spike on her shield boss almost as effectively as she used her sword!

'What women we are!' cried Ilian. 'What fighters!'

She saw how disconcerted the enemy warriors were to discover the number of women who had come against them. There were few worlds, it seemed, where women fought like men. It had never been so on Garathorm, before the coming of Katinka van Bak.

Ilian saw Mysenal of Hinn grin briefly at her, his eyes shining as he rode past her towards a cluster of Ymryl's warriors whose retreat had been cut off by three or four flame-lance beams darting from the tops of nearby houses.

Two or three buildings had been ignited by the power weapons and smoke was beginning to curl through the streets. For a moment Ilian was half-blinded and found herself coughing as the acrid stuff entered her throat. Then she was through the cloud and joining Mysenal in his attack on the enemy.

Though she now bled from a dozen minor cuts and grazes, Ilian was tireless. She unhorsed one rider with a blow of her buckler and in the same movement swept her sword round to take a green-furred dwarf through the roof of his gaping mouth so that the point ran deep into his brain. As the dwarf fell, Ilian twisted the sword from his corpse in time to parry an axe which had been thrown at her by a warrior in purple armour whose pointed steel teeth clashed as he tried to draw back his arm to thrust at her with the lance he held in his other hand. Ilian leaned out in her saddle and sliced the hand from the wrist so that fist and spear dropped to the ground. The stump, spouting blood, continued the motion of casting the spear and only then did the warrior with the steel teeth realise what had happened to him and he moaned. But Ilian was riding past him, to where one of her girl warriors stood over the corpse of her dead *vayna* desperately trying to ward off the blows of three men with reptilian skins (but who were otherwise dressed dissimilarly) who were determined to slay her. Ilian clove the skull of one reptile man, smashed another unconscious so that he fell backward across his horse's rump, and pierced the heart of the last, clearing a way for the girl who darted her a quick smile of gratitude before picking up her flame-lance and running for an open doorway.

And then Ilian was in the square with a score of her warriors at her back and she called out jubilantly:

'We are through!'

Men on foot came running from every house then, those who had not taken part in the cavalry charge, and soon Ilian was surrounded again.

And soon Ilian was laughing again, as life after life was extinguished by her sparkling sword.

The sun was setting.

Ilian cried to her warriors. 'Hasten now! Let us finish this before the night falls and makes our work more difficult.'

The remnants of the enemy cavalry had been driven back into the square. The remnants of the infantry were falling back towards the great house, the house Ymryl had called his 'palace' and where Ilian had been born. It was also the house where she had shuddered, screamed and called out the hiding place of her brother.

For a moment Ilian's joy was replaced by a feeling of black despair, and she paused. The sounds of the battle seemed to fade. The whole scene became remote. And she remembered the face of Ymryl, almost boyish in seriousness, leaning forward and saying to her: 'Where is he? Where is Bradne?'

And she had told him.

Ilian shuddered. She lowered her sword, oblivious to the danger which still threatened her from all sides. Five warped creatures, their bodies and faces covered in huge warts, flung themselves upwards at her, hands clutching. She felt sharp nails dig through the links of her mail. She looked at them absently.

'Bradne . . .' she murmured.

'Are you wounded, girl!' Katinka van Bak appeared, and an axe bit into a skull, a mace crunched into a shoulder. The warted ones squealed. 'Are you dazed?'

Ilian forced herself from the trance, using her own sword to hack down a wart-covered body. 'Only for a moment,' she said.

'There's about a hundred left!' Katinka van Bak said. 'They've barricaded themselves in your father's mansion. I doubt if we'll have winkled them out before nightfall.'

'Then we must fire the building,' said Ilian coldly. 'We must burn them.'

Katinka frowned. 'I like not that. Even these should have the opportunity to surrender . . .'

'Burn them and burn the building. Burn it!' Ilian

wheeled her *vayna* about to look around the square. It
was piled with corpses. About fifty of her own folk still
remained alive. 'It will save more fighting, will it not,
Katinka van Bak?'

'It will, but . . .'

'And spare the lives of some of our folk who still
survive?'

'Aye . . .' Katinka tried to meet Ilian's eyes, but Ilian
turned her face away. 'Aye. But what of the building
itself. Your ancestors have dwelled in it for generations.
It is the finest building in all Virinthorm. There's scarcely a finer in the whole of Garathorm. The woods of its
construction are rare. Many of the varieties of tree which
went to build it are now extinct . . .'

'Let it burn. I could not live there again.'

Katinka sighed. 'I will give the order, though it's not
to my liking. Cannot I offer our enemies a chance to
surrender to us?'

'They gave us no such chance.'

'But we are not them. Morally . . .'

'I'll hear nothing of morality for the moment, thank
you.'

Katinka van Bak rode to do Queen Ilian's bidding.

CHAPTER TWO

AN IMPOSSIBLE DEATH

They were grim-faced, those men and women, as they stood with their hands resting on their weapons, their faces stained red by the firelight, and watched Pyran's mansion burning in the blackness of the night, smelled the smell which came from the pyre, listened to the thin, horrible sounds that still issued through the thick, black smoke from time to time.

'It is just,' said Ilian of Garathorm.

'But there are other forms of justice,' said Katinka van Bak in a quiet voice. 'You cannot burn away the guilt you feel, Ilian.'

'Can I not, madam?' Ilian laughed harshly. 'Yet how do you explain the satisfaction I feel?'

'I am not used to this,' said Katinka van Bak. She spoke for Ilian's ears alone; she spoke reluctantly. 'I've witnessed such acts of vengeance before, yet I like not the sense of unease I feel now. You have become cruel, Ilian.'

'It is ever the fate of the Champion,' said another voice. It was Jhary's. 'Ever. Do not fret, Katinka van Bak. The Champion must always seek to rid himself— or herself—of a certain ambiguous burden. And one of the means the Champion employs is deliberate cruelty —actions which go against the dictates of the Champion's conscience. Ilian thinks she bears only the guilt

of her brother's betrayal. It is not so. It is a guilt which
you and I, Katinka van Bak, could never experience.
And we should thank all our gods for that!'

Ilian shuddered. She had barely heard Jhary's words,
but she was disturbed by their import.

With a shrug, Katinka van Bak turned away. 'As
you say, Jhary. You know more of such matters than
do I. And there would be no Ilian at all to fight Ymryl
if it were not for your knowledge.' She stalked off into
the smoky shadows.

Jhary stood beside Ilian for a while. Then he, too,
left her alone, staring into the blazing ruins of her old
home.

The cries died and the stink of burning flesh faded
until the sweet odours of the wood became predomin-
ant. Ilian felt drained of life. And as the blaze sub-
sided, she moved closer, as if seeking warmth, for there
was an awful chill in her bones now, though the night
was not cold.

Still she saw Ymryl's sober features asking her that
question. Still she heard her own voice replying.

When Jhary found her it was close to dawn and she
was trampling through the blackened bones, the cinders
and the hot ash, kicking at a charred skull here and a
broken rib cage there.

'News,' said Jhary.

She looked out at him through her bleak eyes.

'News of Ymryl. He was successful in his war. He
has slain Arnald and has heard what happened here
last night. He's returning.'

Ilian drew deeply of the acrid air. 'Then we must
prepare,' she said.

'With half our force remaining, we shall be hard-
pressed to stand against Ymryl's army. He now has

Arnald's strength, also—or what remains of it. At least two thousand warriors come against us! Perhaps it would be better tactics to return to the trees, harry them from time to time . . .'

'We shall continue with the plan we originally devised,' said Ilian.

Jhary-a-Conel shrugged. 'Very well.'

'Have Ymryl's flame-cannon been found?'

'They have. Hidden in cellars in a wine-press west of here. And Katinka van Bak saw that they were set up in a defensive ring during the night. Others are mounted to cover each of the main thoroughfares into the centre of the city. It is as well we acted swiftly. I for one did not expect Ymryl to return so soon.'

Ilian began to wade through the ashes. 'Katinka van Bak is an experienced general.'

'We are lucky that she is,' said Jhary.

Soon after midday the scouts came back with news that Ymryl was using similar tactics to Ilian's in approaching the city, closing in from all sides. Ilian prayed that Ymryl's scouts had not seen the hastily concealed flame-cannon. She had put about half her force to operating the power weapons. The others she had positioned in hiding elsewhere.

About an hour later, the first wave of cavalry, all shining armour and fluttering pennants, came thundering down the four broad avenues which led to the city square.

The square itself was apparently deserted, save for the corpses which had been left there.

The cavalry's tempo began to slacken as the first riders saw what lay ahead and became confused.

From somewhere high overhead there came the silvery note of a horn.

And flame-cannon roared.

And where the cavalry had been, in all four quarters, was burning dust, embers drifting in the air, ash settling on the streets.

Ilian, hidden in the trees, smiled, remembering how those same flame-cannon had cut down her own folk.

The odds against her had now been improved by a matter of some several hundred, but the flame-cannon could not be used again, for they had to be filled once more with the substance which fuelled them and that substance required delicate handling and much time was involved in pouring it, drop by drop, into the chambers. Ilian saw those who had operated the cannon spring up and run back to the square, disappearing into buildings.

Silence fell again over Virinthorm.

Then, from the west, came a clattering of hooves. The leaf-filtered sunlight flashed on jeweled masks, on bright horse-armour.

From her own position in a tree some hundred yards away, Katinka van Bak called:

'It is Kalan and a Dark Empire force. They have flame weapons, too.'

Baron Kalan's snake mask glittered as he rode at headlong speed down the broad avenue. From the houses came the thin, red beams of light, issuing from Ilian's remaining flame-lances. Several of the beams seemed to pass through Kalan's body without harming him and Ilian thought that her eyes deceived her. Even the sorcerer could not be impervious to those deadly beams.

Others fell, however, before their comrades had time to return the fire, aiming their flame-lances at random in the general direction of the houses from

which the attacks had come until the air was a lattice of
ruby rays.

And still Kalan rode straight for the square, his
horse panting as he spurred it until its blood spurted
from its flanks.

Kalan was laughing. It was a laugh that was familiar
to Ilian and she could not place it for a moment until
she remembered that it was not unlike that laughter she
had herself shouted during the previous day's battle.

Kalan rode until he came to the square and then his
laughter gave way to a wail of rage as he saw the remains of the great mansion.

'My laboratories!'

He dismounted from his horse and walked into the
ruins, staring about him, oblivious to any danger which
might threaten him, while behind him his men fought a
fierce battle with Ilian's warriors who had emerged from
the houses and were engaging them hand to hand.

Ilian watched him. She was fascinated. What did he
seek?

Two of Ilian's warriors detached themselves from the
main party and came running at Kalan. He turned when
he heard them and again he laughed, drawing his sword.
The laughter echoed eerily in his snake helm.

'Leave me alone,' he called to the warriors. 'You
cannot harm me.'

And now Ilian gasped. She saw one of the warriors
thrust his sword into Kalan. She saw the point emerge
on the other side of the sorcerer's body. She saw Kalan
back away, slashing at his attacker with his own sword,
cutting a deep wound in the man's shoulder. But Kalan
was unwounded. The warrior groaned. Impatiently,
Kalan drove his sword into the warrior's throat so that
he dropped into the ashes of the mansion. The other
warrior hesitated before striking at Baron Kalan, driv-

ing at the Dark Empire Lord's unarmoured forearm.
It was a blow which should have shorn the limb from
Kalan, but again Kalan was completely unhurt. At this
the warrior backed off. Ignoring him, Kalan continued
his frantic search amongst the charred corpses and the
embers, calling back to the warrior:

'I cannot be slain. Do not waste my time and I shall
not waste yours. There is something I seek here. What
fool can have wrought such unnecessary destruction?'
And when the warrior remained where he was, the
serpent helm lifted and Kalan said, as if explaining to a
stupid child: 'I cannot be slain. There is only one man
who can slay me in all the infinite cosmos. And I do not
see him here. Begone!'

Ilian sympathised with her warrior as she watched
him stumble away.

And then Kalan chuckled. 'I have it!' He bent and
picked something from the dust.

Ilian swung down from the trees and dropped into
the square, confronting Kalan across a sea of corpses.

'Baron Kalan?'

He looked up. 'I have it . . .' He made to show it to
her and then he hesitated. 'What? It cannot be! Have
all my powers deserted me, then?'

'You thought you had slain me?' Ilian began to ad-
vance towards him. She had seen that he was invul-
nerable, yet she felt she had to confront him, for she
was moved by another of those strange impulses she
could not explain. 'Ilian of Garathorm?'

'Slain? Nonsense. It was much subtler. The jewel ate
your soul. It was my finest creation of that sort, more
sophisticated than anything else I have invented. It was
meant for someone much more important than you, but
the situation demanded that I use it, if I was not to die
by Ymryl's hand.'

From the distance now came the sounds of battle. Ilian knew that her folk were engaging Ymryl's army. Her step did not falter as she continued to walk towards Kalan.

'I have much to avenge myself for on you, Baron Kalan,' she said.

'You cannot kill me, madam, if that's what you mean,' he told her. '*You* cannot do that.'

'But I must try.'

The Serpent Lord shrugged. 'If you must. But I would rather know how your soul escaped from my gem. I had every indication that it was trapped there for eternity. And with such a gem I could have pursued still more complicated experiments. How did it escape?'

Someone called across from the far side of the square. 'It did not, Baron Kalan. It did not escape!' It was Jhary-a-Conel's voice.

The serpent mask turned. 'What do you mean?'

'Did you not understand the nature of the soul you sought to imprison in your gem?'

'Nature? How——?'

'Do you know the legend of the Champion Eternal?'

'I have read something of it, aye . . .' The serpent mask turned from Jhary to Ilian, from Ilian to Jhary. And still Ilian continued to pace toward Baron Kalan.

'Then recall what you read.'

And Ilian stood before Baron Kalan of Vitall and with a movement of her sword she had swept the serpent helm from his shoulders to reveal his pale, middle-aged face with its whispy white beard, its thinning hair. Kalan blinked and made to cover his face, then he dropped his hands to his side, his sword hanging by its wrist-thong, one fist bunched around the thing he had sought among the ruins.

Kalan said softly: 'You still cannot slay me, Ilian of

Garathorm. And even if you could, it would result in terrible consequences. Let me go. Or hold me prisoner, if you like. I have matters to consider . . .'

'Put up your sword, Baron Kalan, and defend yourself.'

'I would be reluctant to slay you,' said Kalan, his voice becoming harsher, 'for you offer an intriguing mystery to a man of science, but I *shall* kill you, Ilian, if you continue to plague me.'

'And I shall kill you, if I can.'

'I told you,' said Kalan reasonably, 'that I can only be slain by one creature in the entire multiverse. And that creature is not yourself. Besides, more than you realise depends upon my remaining alive . . .'

'Defend yourself!'

Kalan shrugged and held up his sword.

Ilian thrust. Kalan parried carelessly. Her blade continued on its course, deflected only a fraction, and her point entered his flesh. Kalan's eyes widened.

'Pain!' he hissed in astonishment. 'It is pain!'

Ilian was almost as surprised as Kalan to see the blood flowing. Kalan staggered back, looking down at his wound. 'It is not possible,' he said firmly. 'It is not.'

And Ilian thrust again, this time striking directly at his heart as Kalan said: 'Only Hawkmoon can kill me. Only he. It is impossible . . .'

And he fell backwards in the ashes, causing a small cloud of black dust to spurt up around him. The look of astonishment was still printed on his dead features.

'Now we are both avenged, Baron Kalan,' said Ilian in a voice she did not recognise as her own.

She bent to see what the baron had clutched in his hand, prying it from the fingers.

It was something which gleamed like polished coal. An irregularly cut gem. She knew what it must be.

As she straightened up she noticed that the quality of the light around her had altered subtly. It was as if clouds had passed around the sun, yet the rains were not due yet for another two months.

Jhary-a-Conel came running towards her. 'So you did slay him! But I fear that action will bring more trouble to us.' He glanced at the gem she held. 'Keep that safely. If we come through this together, I will show you what you must do with it.'

Overhead, in the darkening sky, through the topmost branches of Garathorm's massive trees, there came a sound. It was like the beating of the wings of a gigantic bird. And there was a stink, too, that made the smell of the corpses seem sweet in comparison.

'What is it, Jhary?' Ilian felt fear filling her whole mind. She wanted to flee from the thing which was coming to Virinthorm.

'Kalan warned you that there would be consequences if he was slain here. You see, his experiments created the disruptions in the whole balance of the multiverse. By slaying him you have enabled the multiverse to begin healing itself, though that will bring further disruptions of what some would call a minor nature.'

'But what causes that sound, that smell?'

'Listen,' said Jhary-a-Conel. 'Do you hear anything else.'

Ilian listened carefully. In the distance she could hear the barking note of a war-horn. Ymryl's horn.

'He has summoned Arioch, Lord of Chaos,' said Jhary. 'And Kalan's dying has enabled Arioch to break through at last. Ymryl has a new ally, Ilian.'

CHAPTER THREE

THE SWAYING OF THE BALANCE

Jhary was full of a wild, despairing mirth as he mounted his yellow horse, casting many glances at the sky. It was still dark, but the sound of that awful flapping had gone and the stink had faded.

'Only you, Jhary, know what we fight now,' said Katinka van Bak soberly. She wiped sweat from her face with her sleeve, the sword still in her hand.

Yisselda of Brass rode up. On her arm was a long, shallow cut. The blood had congealed in the wound.

'Ymryl has withdrawn his attack,' she said. 'I cannot determine what strategy he plans . . .' Her voice tailed off as she saw Kalan's corpse still lying in the ashes. 'So,' she said, 'he is dead. Good. He had the superstition, you know, that he could only be slain by my husband, Hawkmoon.'

Katinka van Bak almost smiled. 'Aye,' she said. 'I know.'

'Have you any thought as to what Ymryl plans next?' Yisselda asked Katinka van Bak.

'He has little need of strategy now, according to what Jhary tells us,' the warrior woman replied wearily. 'He has demons aiding him now!'

'You are choosing the terminology to suit your own prejudices,' said Jhary-a-Conel. 'If I called Arioch a being of considerably advanced mental and physical powers, you would accept his existence completely.'

'I accept his existence, anyway!' snorted Katinka van Bak. 'I have heard him. I have sniffed him!'

'Well,' said Ilian in a small voice, 'we must continue our fight with Ymryl, even if it is doomed. Shall we continue our defensive strategy or alter it to one of attack?'

'It scarcely matters now,' said Jhary-a-Conel, 'but it would be nobler to die in an attack, would it not?' He smiled to himself. 'Strange how death remains unwelcome, for all I understand my fate.'

They moved through the trees, their mounts abandoned. They were stealthy and they carried the flame-lances they had taken from the dead Dark Empire warriors whom Kalan had led.

Jhary led them and now he paused, raising his hand as he looked down through the leaves, wrinkling his nose.

They saw Ymryl's camp. He had made it on the very edge of the city. They saw Ymryl, his yellow horn bouncing on his naked chest. He wore only a pair of silken breeks and his feet were unshod. His arms were bound about with bracelets of leather studded with jewels and he had a broad leather belt round his waist, which carried his heavy broadsword, his broad-bladed dirk and a weapon which could shoot tiny, squat arrows across long distances. His great untidy mop of yellow hair fell across his face and his uneven teeth gleamed as he grinned somewhat nervously at his new ally.

His ally was about nine feet tall and about six feet broad with a dark, scaly skin. It was naked, hermaphrodite, and there was a pair of leathery wings folded on

its back. It seemed to be in some pain as it moved
about, gnawing hungrily at the remains of one of Ymryl's soldiers.

But the unnerving thing about Ymryl's ally was its
face. It was a face which kept changing. At one moment
it would be repulsively bestial and ugly, at another it
would become the face of a beautiful youth. Only the
eyes, the pain-racked eyes, did not change. Occasionally, however, they flashed with intelligence, but for the
most part were cruel, fierce, primitive.

Ymryl's voice trembled, but it was triumphant. 'You
will aid me now, will you not, Lord Arioch. It was the
bargain we made . . .'

'Aye, the bargain,' grunted the demon. 'I have made
so many. And so many have reneged of late . . .'

'I am still loyal to you, my lord.'

'I am under attack myself. Huge forces come against
me on many planes, in many times. Men disrupt the
multiverse. The balance has gone! The balance has
gone! Chaos crumbles and Law is no more . . .'

Arioch seemed to be speaking more to himself than
to Ymryl.

Ymryl said hesitantly: 'But your power? You still
have your power?'

'Aye, much of it. Oh, I can aid you in your business
here, Ymryl, for as long as it should last.'

'Last? What mean you, my Lord Arioch?'

But Arioch chewed the meat from the last bone and
threw it down, dragging himself across the ground to
peer towards the centre of the city.

Ilian shivered as she saw the face change to become
fat, fleshy, jowelled, the teeth rotting. The lips moved
as Arioch murmured to himself. *'It is a matter of per-
spective, Corum. We follow our whims . . .'* Arioch
scowled. *'Ah, Elric, sweetest of my slaves . . . all turn-*

ing—all turning. What means it?' And the features
changed again, to become the features of a handsome
boy. *'The planes intersect, the balance tilts, the old
battles become obscure, the old ways are no more. Do
the gods truly die? Can the gods die?'*

And, for all she loathed the monster, Ilian felt a
peculiar pang of sympathy for Arioch as she overheard
his musings.

'How shall we strike, great Arioch?' Ymryl stepped
up to his supernatural master. 'Will you lead us?'

'Lead you? It is not my way to lead mortals into
battle. Ah!' Arioch let out a scream of agony. 'I cannot
remain here!'

'You must, Arioch! Our bargain!'

'Yes, Ymryl, our bargain. I gave you the horn, that
which is brother to the Horn of Fate. And there are so
few still loyal to the Chaos Lords, so few worlds where
we still survive . . .'

'Then you will give us power?'

Again Arioch's face changed, back to its primitive,
demonic form. And Arioch growled, all the intelligence
disappearing from his face. And he drew deep, snorting
breaths, and his body began to change colour, to grow
in size, to flare with reds and yellows as if a mighty
furnace roared within him.

'He gathers his strength,' whispered Jhary-a-Conel,
his lips close to Ilian's ear. 'We must strike now. Now,
Ilian.'

He leapt, his flame-lance sending out its stream of
ruby light. He jumped into the ranks of the great army
and four warriors were cut down before any realised
that an enemy had come among them. Now others of
Ilian's warriors dropped from the trees, following
Jhary's example. Katinka van Bak, Yisselda of Brass,
Lyfeth of Ghant, Mysenal of Hinn—all jumped into the

fray, jumped to certain death. And Ilian wondered why she hung back.

She saw Ymryl yell urgently at Arioch, saw Arioch reach out to touch Ymryl. Ymryl's body glowed, seeming to burn with the same fire which filled Arioch.

And Ymryl screamed, drawing his sword, and rushing upon Ilian's handful of warriors.

That was when Ilian jumped, placing herself between her folk and Ymryl.

Ymryl was possessed. His form radiated a monstrous energy as if Arioch himself possessed that mortal body. Ymryl's eyes, even, were the bestial eyes of Arioch. He snarled. He came at Ilian with his great sword hissing through the air. 'Ah, now, Ilian. This time you shall die. This time!'

And Ilian tried to block the blow, but so strong had Ymryl become that her sword was driven back against her body. She stumbled backward, again barely able to ward off Ymryl's next swipe at her. He fought with reasonless ferocity and she knew that he must kill her.

And behind Ymryl, Arioch had grown to huge proportions. His body continued to writhe, growing larger and larger, but containing less and less substance. The face altered constantly now, from second to second, and she heard a faint voice calling:

'The balance! The balance! It sways! It bends! It melts! It is the doom of the gods! Oh, these puny creatures—these men . . .'

And then Arioch was gone and only Ymryl was left, but an Ymryl filled with Arioch's terrible power.

Ilian continued to retreat before the rain of blows. Her arms were aching. Her legs and her back were aching. She was afraid. She did not want Ymryl to kill her.

Somewhere she heard another sound. Was it a yell

of triumph? Did it mean that all her comrades were dead now, that Ymryl's soldiers had destroyed every one of them?

Was she the last of Garathorm?

She fell back as, with a terrific blow, Ymryl knocked the sword from her hand. Another blow split her buckler. Ymryl drew back his arm to deliver the death stroke.

CHAPTER FOUR

THE SOUL GEM

Ilian tried to stare Ymryl in his eyes as she died, those eyes which were no longer his own, but Arioch's.

But then the light in them began to fade and Ymryl looked about him in wonder. She heard him say:

'It is over, then? We go home?'

He seemed to be looking at scenery that was not the scenery of Garathorm. And he was smiling.

Ilian reached out and her hand grasped the hilt of her sword. With all her strength she thrust out at Ymryl and she saw his blood spurt, his face become astonished, as gradually he faded into nothingness, as Arioch had faded before him.

Dazed, Ilian staggered upright, not knowing if she had killed Ymryl. Now she would never know.

Katinka van Bak lay nearby. She had a great, red wound in her body. Her face was white as if all her blood had gone. She was panting. As Ilian approached her, Katinka said:

'I heard the story of Hawkmoon's sword—the Sword of the Dawn it was called. It could summon warriors from another plane, another time. Could some other sword have summoned Ymryl . . .?' She hardly knew what she was saying.

Jhary-a-Conel, supported by Yisselda of Brass, came

limping out of the battle-dust. His leg was cut, but not deeply.

'So you saved us, after all, Ilian,' he said. 'As the Eternal Champion should!' He grinned. 'But does not, I'll admit, always do . . .'

'I saved you? No. I cannot explain this. Ymryl vanished!'

'You slew Kalan. It was Kalan who had created the circumstances which allowed Ymryl and the rest to come to Garathorm. With Kalan's death the rift in the multiverse begins to mend. In healing itself, it replaces Ymryl and all who served Ymryl back in their respective eras. I'm sure that's what happened. These are strange times, Ilian of Garathorm. Almost as strange for me as they are for you. I'm used to gods exerting their will—but Arioch—he is wretched now. Do the gods die in all planes, I wonder?'

'There have never been gods on Garathorm,' said Ilian. She bent to attend Katinka van Bak's wound, hoping that it was not as serious as it looked. But it was worse than it looked. Katinka van Bak was dying.

'They have all gone, then?' said Yisselda, hardly realising, still, that their friend was so badly wounded.

'All—including corpses,' said Jhary. He was fumbling in the pouch at his belt. 'This will help her,' he said. 'A potion to kill pain.'

Ilian put the vial to Katinka van Bak's lips, but the warrior woman shook her head. 'No,' she said, 'it will make me sleep. I want to remain awake for what little life I have left. And I must go home.'

'Home? To Virinthorm?' said Ilian softly.

'No. To my own home. Back through the Bulgar Mountains.' Katinka sought with her eyes for Jhary-a-Conel. 'Will you take me there, Jhary?'

'We must have a litter,' he said. He called to Lyfeth,

who had come up. 'Can some of your folk make a litter?'

Ilian said absently, 'You are all still alive? But how? I thought you went to your deaths . . .?'

'The sea-folk!' said Lyfeth as she went away to help make the litter. 'Did you not see them?'

'The sea-folk? My attention was on that demon . . .'

'Just as Jhary leapt down into their camp, we saw their banners. That was why we chose to attack when we did. Look!'

Moving towards the trees to cut branches, Lyfeth pointed.

And Ilian smiled with pleasure as she saw the warriors there, each armed with a great harpoon-gun, each mounted on huge seal-like creatures. On only a few occasions had she seen the sea-folk, but she knew that they were proud and that they were strong, hunting the whales of the sea upon their amphibious beasts.

While Yisselda dressed Katinka van Bak's wounds, Ilian went to thank King Treshon, their leader.

He dismounted and bowed graciously. 'My lady,' he said. 'My queen.' Though an old man, he was still very fit and muscles rippled on his bronzed body. He wore a sleeveless mail shirt and a leather kilt, just as all his warriors did. 'Now we can make Garathorm live again.'

'Did you know of our battle?'

'No. We had spies watching Arnald of Grovent—he who finally became leader of those who took our towns. When he set off to march against Ymryl, we decided that it was the best time to strike—while they were divided and concentrating on attack from other quarters—'

'Just as we did!' Ilian said. 'It is happy for both of us that we decided upon the same strategy.'

'We were well-advised,' said King Treshon.

'Advised? By whom?'

'By yonder youth . . .' King Treshon indicated Jhary-a-Conel who was sitting next to Katinka van Bak and conversing with her in a low voice. 'He visited us a month or so since and outlined the plan we followed.'

Ilian smiled. 'He knows much, that youth.'

'Aye, my lady.'

Ilian reached into her belt purse and felt the hard edges of the black jewel. She was in a reflective mood as she trudged back to where Jhary sat, having taken her leave of King Treshon for the moment.

'You told me to keep the jewel safe,' she said. She took it from her purse, holding it up. 'Here it is.'

'I am glad it is still here,' said Jhary. 'I feared it would be whisked back to wherever Kalan's corpse now lies!'

'You planned much of what has happened here, Jhary-a-Conel, did you not?'

'Plan it? No. I serve, that is all. I do what must be done.' Jhary was pale. She noticed that he was trembling.

'What's ill? Did you sustain a worse wound than we thought?'

'No. But those forces which pulled Arioch and Ymryl from your world also demand that I leave, it seems. We must make haste to the cave.'

'The cave?'

'Where we first met.' Jhary got up and ran towards his yellow horse. 'Mount whatever there is to ride. Have two of your warriors bear Katinka's litter. Bring Yisselda of Brass with you. Quickly, to the cave!' And he was already riding.

Ilian saw that the litter was almost ready. She told Yisselda what Jhary had said and they went to find mounts.

'But why am I still in this world?' Yisselda said,

frowning. 'Should not I have returned to the world where Kalan held me prisoner?'

'You feel nothing—nothing pulling you from here?' Ilian said.

'Nothing.'

Impulsively Ilian reached forward and kissed Yisselda lightly on the cheek. 'Farewell,' she said.

Yisselda was surprised. 'You do not come with us to the cave?'

'I come with you. But I wished to say goodbye. I cannot explain why.'

Ilian felt a mood of peace begin to descend on her. Again she touched the black jewel in her pouch. She smiled.

Jhary was standing in the cave-mouth when they arrived. He looked even weaker than before. He held his black and white cat tightly to his chest.

'Ah,' he said. 'I thought I would not be here. Good.'

Lyfeth of Ghant and Mysenal of Hinn had insisted on carrying Katinka van Bak's litter themselves. They made to carry it into the cave, but Jhary stopped them. 'I am sorry,' he said. 'You must wait here. If Ilian does not return, you must elect a new ruler in her place.'

'A new ruler? What do you intend to do with her?' Mysenal leapt forward, hand on his sword. 'What harm can befall her in that cave?'

'No harm. But Kalan's jewel still contains her soul . . .' Jhary was sweating. He gasped and shook his head. 'I cannot explain now. Be assured I will protect your queen . . .'

And he followed Yisselda and Ilian, who were now carrying Katinka van Bak's litter, into the cave.

Ilian was astonished at how deep the cave was. It seemed to go on and on into the mountainside. And it became colder as they went deeper. Yet she said nothing, trusting Jhary.

She turned only once, when she heard Mysenal's excited voice in the distance, shouting: 'We blame you for nothing, now, Ilian! You are absolved . . .'

And she wondered at Mysenal's tone and why he should feel such urgency in expressing that sentiment. Not that it meant a great deal to her. She knew her guilt, whatever others said.

And then Katinka van Bak said weakly from her litter, 'Is this not the spot, Jhary-a-Conel?'

Jhary nodded. Since the light had faded, he had carried an odd globe in his hand—a globe which gleamed with light. He set this down upon the floor of the cavern and then Ilian gasped at what she saw. It was the corpse of a tall and handsome man, dressed all in furs. There was no wound on his body, nothing to indicate how he had died. And his face reminded her of someone's. She closed her eyes. 'Hawkmoon . . .' she murmured. 'My name . . .'

Yisselda was sobbing as she knelt down beside the corpse.

'Dorian! My love! My love!' She turned to look up at Jhary-a-Conel. 'Why did you not warn me of this?'

Jhary ignored her and turned instead to Ilian who was leaning dazedly against the wall of the cave. 'Give me the jewel,' he said. 'The black jewel, Ilian. Give it to me.'

And when Ilian felt for the gem in her purse she found something that was warm, that vibrated.

'It is alive!' she said. 'Alive!'

'Aye.' He spoke urgently in a low, thin voice. 'Hurry. Kneel beside him . . .'

'The corpse?' Ilian drew back distastefully.

'Do as I say!' Jhary weakly dragged Yisselda back

from Hawkmoon's body and made Ilian kneel. She did
so reluctantly. 'Now, place the jewel upon his forehead—place it where you see the scar.'

Trembling, she did as he ordered.

'Place your own forehead against the gem.'

She bent and her forehead touched the pulsing jewel
and suddenly she was falling *into* the jewel and *through*
the jewel, and as she fell, someone else fell towards her
—as if she fell towards a mirror image of herself. She
cried out . . .

She heard Jhary's weak 'Farewell!' and she tried to
answer, but she could not. On and on she fell, through
corridors of sensations, of memories, of guilt and of
redemption . . .

And she was Asquiol and she was Arflane and she
was Alaric. She was John Daker, Erekosë and Urlik.
She was Corum and Elric and she was Hawkmoon . . .

'Hawkmoon!' she cried the name with her own lips
and it was a battle-cry. She fought Baron Meliadus and
Asrovaak Mikosevaar at the Battle of the Kamarg. She
fought Meliadus again at Londra and Yisselda was beside her. And she and Yisselda looked upon the battle-
field when it was all over and they saw that of their
comrades only they survived . . .

'Yisselda!'

'I am here, Dorian. I am here!'

He opened his eyes and he said: 'So Katinka van Bak
did not betray me! But what a devious ruse to bring me
to you. Why should she concoct so complicated a
scheme?'

Katinka whispered from her litter. 'Perhaps you will
find out one day, but not from me, for I save my
breath. I need you two to take me out of these mountains, to Ukrainia where I wish to die.'

Hawkmoon got up. He was horribly stiff, as if he

had lain in the same spot for months. He saw the blood on the bandages. 'You are wounded! I did not strike out. At least, I cannot recall . . .' He put his hand to his forehead. There was something warm there, like blood, but when he drew his fingers away there was only a faint, dark radiance which flickered for a moment before it vanished. 'Then how—Jherek? Surely not . . .'

Katinka van Bak smiled. 'No. Yisselda will tell you how I got this.'

Another woman said in a soft and vibrant voice from behind Hawkmoon, 'She sustained her wound helping to save a country that was not her own.'

'Not for the first time has she been wounded thus,' said Hawkmoon turning. He stared at a face of extraordinary beauty and yet it was a face that had a sadness in it. A sadness that he felt he might define if he thought for a moment. 'We have met before?'

'You have met before,' said Katinka, 'but now you must part swiftly, for there will be other disruptions if you occupy the same plane for much longer. Believe my warning, Ilian of Garathorm. Go back now. Go back to Mysenal and Lyfeth. They will help you restore your country.'

'But . . .' Ilian hesitated. 'I would speak longer with Yisselda and this Hawkmoon.'

'You have not the right. You are two aspects of the same thing. Only on certain occasions can you meet. Jhary told me that. Go back. Hurry!'

Reluctantly the beautiful girl turned, her golden hair swinging, her chain-mail clinking. She began to walk into the darkness and soon she had vanished from sight.

'Where does the tunnel lead, Katinka van Bak,' Hawkmoon asked, 'to Ukrainia?'

'Not to Ukrainia. And soon it will lead to nowhere at all. I hope she fares well, that maid. She has much to do. And I have a feeling that she will meet Ymryl again.'

'Ymryl?'

Katinka van Bak sighed. 'I told you I would not waste my breath. I need it to keep me alive until we reach Ukrainia. Let us hope the sleigh still waits for us below.'

And Hawkmoon shrugged. He turned to look tenderly upon Yisselda. 'I knew you lived,' he said. 'They called me mad. But I knew you lived.'

They embraced. 'Oh, Dorian, such adventures I have had,' said Yisselda.

'Tell him about them later,' said the dying Katinka van Bak pettishly from her litter. 'Now pick up this stretcher and get me to that sleigh!'

As she stooped to take one end of the litter, Yisselda said: 'And how do the children fare, Dorian?'

And she wondered why Hawkmoon continued the rest of the journey through the tunnel in silence.

This ends the Second of the Chronicles of Castle Brass